THE QUALITIES
of a
GOOD CITIZEN

ESSENTIAL PILLARS
OF NATION-BUILDING

Sunday Jial

Africa
World Books
Pty Ltd

A Note from the Publisher

The publisher wishes to acknowledge and thank Dr Douglas H. Johnson for his invaluable help and support for Africa World Books and its mission of preserving and promoting African cultural and literary traditions and history. Dr Johnson and fellow historians have been instrumental in ensuring that African people remain connected to their past and their identity. Africa World Books is proud to carry on this mission.

© William Sunday Jial, 2020

ISBN: 978-0-6488415-9-3

Design and typesetting: Africa World Books

Dedication

To my father Simon Jial and his colleagues who fought earnestly during the three phases of the liberation struggle, starting from Anya-Nya I, Anya-Nya II, and the SPLA, but did not complete the travailing journey to independence alive in order to see the result of their effort or enjoy the fruits of their labor. This book is the prize of their lifelong sacrifice.

Acknowledgments

I HAVE TO START by thanking my awesome and courageous mother, Mary, who together with my late father, Jial, crossed numerous rivers, deserts, and surreal international borders in search of a place where I could pursue my basic education. These two legends taught me respect, discipline, love, manners, honesty, fear of God, and so much more that has helped me succeed in life today. In their generation, they were able to envision a bright future for an innocent and carefree child. Mommy and Daddy, thank you so much. I cannot thank you enough.

To my children, Muc, Pal, and Jial Jr., I don't have a word for you, sons. You made enormous contributions to this book. Little did you know that your brilliant smiles and jokes helped reduce my stress and generated more positive emotions within me during this project. These smiles enabled me to connect letters, words, sentences, and chapters of what people call a book today. Although there were many vicissitudes during this writing process as I was trying to balance work, family, and writing, your smiles took me the extra miles to accomplish the annual goal I set for myself. Thank you, sons — you mean the world to me.

To my entire family and all those who stood by me during all my struggles, failures, and successes, I am perpetually grateful to all of you. Writing a book requires peace of mind, as an interrupted and stressed subconscious mind hardly produces clean thoughts. All of you understood my utmost desire for a peaceful mind, and throughout this journey, I was able to enjoy tranquility on a silver plate. Thank you so much for being part of my life.

Contents

Prologue

A GOOD CITIZEN IS A GODSEND and venerated by society the world over. The utmost civil power has certain responsibilities towards us, and for this reason, we must realize that we have the same responsibility toward the state to which we belong. To achieve this, we must first be aware of both our duties and freedoms in every step we take in life, because in any country, there are established duties that every citizen is obliged to follow. In view of this, we should consider our duties more than what the term itself has to offer, and this can only be possible when our actions reflect our morals.

Good citizenship qualities can be inculcated in people at any stage of life, from infancy to old age. This is why in 1805, Napoleon I said, "If the child is not taught from infancy that he ought to be a republican or a monarchist, a Catholic or a free-thinker, the state will not constitute a nation; it will rest on uncertain and shifting foundations; and it will be constantly exposed to disorder and change."

When I published my first book, titled Living Your Life Impeccably, I presumed that I had done my part as a citizen to contribute to the nation-building in the republic. However, one year later, I realized that the book was just the beginning and not the end of my contribution. I am also convinced that a heterogeneous state of South Sudan requires more than just a hit and halt contribution.

While I am certain that the morals of the country and its brainpower have seen massive improvement since the referendum, declaration of independence, and formation of the Constitution, I have yet to see any great improvement in public spirit and volunteering, compassion, respect for diversity, honesty, tolerance, meaningful nationalism, self-discipline, perfect allegiance to the country, or citizens' compliance to the rule of law.

There is no doubt that we would probably have improved in all social, economic, and political qualities if the civil war had not introduced unimaginable obliteration, which has put the intelligent and the ignorant, the good and the bad, the sane and the insane, the rich and the poor, the young and the old on the same level. Nevertheless, this should not kill our public spirit as a nation, as we have much more to do to change the situation for the better.

A disciplined and hardworking nation always develops and prospers faster than a country with undisciplined and lazy citizens. If we had worked to improve these traits, then by now, I am convinced that we could catch up with and even do better than some countries with low Growth Domestic Product around the world.

In his inaugural address, U.S. President John F. Kennedy urged his compatriots, "Ask not what your country can do for you but what you can do for your country." As a nation, we too need to combat the mindset that sees the government as the sole distributor of all opportunities. It is your responsibility to create an opportunity for yourself. After you do your part, then ask the government to provide roads, security, and healthcare to the population in which you are included. As citizens, we should work hard to cater to our own needs. No matter what job we do, working hard is an important part of being a good citizen.

Being a good citizen is also important in caring for others and improving the community's welfare. To be a good citizen, you need to be responsible for paying your taxes, which in turn helps the government to meet its expenditures and provide important services to the people, especially the vulnerable who cannot provide for their own needs.

For the security and safety of all, every citizen needs to abide by the Constitution and respect its ideals and institutions, including the national flag and the national anthem. More so, as a true citizen, you must cherish and follow the noble ideals that inspired our national struggle for freedom; uphold and protect the sovereignty, unity, and integrity of South Sudan; defend the country and render national service when called upon to do so.

It is also your sole responsibility to promote harmony and the spirit of common brotherhood among the sixty-four tribes of South Sudan while transcending religious, dialectal, regional, tribal, or sectional diversities, including renouncing practices pejorative to the dignity of women and people with special needs.

In the same vein, you also have to value and preserve the rich heritage of our composite culture. We all have a role in protecting and improving the natural environment, including rivers, lakes, forests, and wildlife, while having compassion for all living creatures. We should make it our daily errand to safeguard public property, abjure violence, develop the scientific temper, and inculcate humanism and the spirit of inquiry and reform in the republic.

As parents and/or guardians, we must provide opportunities, particularly education, to our children from childhood until the age of seventeen, when they are prepared enough to cross into adulthood. In fulfillment of this requirement, we need to pay attention to both primary and secondary education and do whatever we can to ensure that our children pursue higher education.

To this end, I am certain that if we all strive toward excellence in all spheres of individual and collective activity, there is nothing that can impede our nation from rising to the higher levels of endeavor and triumph.

ONE

NATIONALISM

"Nations whose nationalism are destroyed are subject to ruin."
Muammar al-Gaddafi

WHEN YOU ARE PROUD OF BEING A CITIZEN of the country you call your own, when you are emotionally attached to it, when you do your part wholeheartedly to help it stay on its intended course, when your loyalty and devotion to your nation surpasses individual, clan or tribal interests, you have already achieved some forms of nationalism. As a true nationalist, you need to celebrate unity with diverse people who share the same values, beliefs, and history of liberation struggle with you. That is why, on the one hand, nationalism is thought of as a method that defines, creates, and expresses essential loyalty to the state, and on the other hand, as a belief, creed, and essentially a political ideology that involves an individual identifying with or becoming attached to one's nation. As the old saying goes, "all roads lead to Rome" — the two definitions above imply that whatever you do to the citizens of your country, be it noble or wicked, you are doing it unto your nation.

To encapsulate the conventional view of the origin and spread of nationalism, we have to admit that it is inherently Western. Nationalism first arose during the Roman Empire, followed by the

Holy Roman Empire. It was geared toward converging nations under a single world-state canopy championed by successive Roman emperors' regimes. This doctrine was later reintroduced in Europe in the eighteenth century and hastily became firmly naturalized in the political rhetoric of the Western world. At the early stage of its reintroduction, it was used as a way to define and promote a nation according to ethnographic principles.

During the eighteenth and nineteenth centuries, revolutions in France and America sparked a new age of nationalism capable of promoting a unified nation characterized by a strong political and economic interest known as capitalism. Since then, nationalism has been considered a driving factor behind everything from radical movements to economics and foreign policy. Nationalism has also focused on preserving a country's culture, language, and shared literature.

Although nationalism was born in Europe, it soon spread to far-flung nations of the world after its acculturation, thus making it a cornerstone of the modern political system across the globe. According to Elie Kedourie, nationalism provides "a criterion for the determination of the unit of population proper to enjoy a government exclusively its own, for the legitimate exercise of power within the state, and for the right organization of a society of states."

To understand nationalism, it is crucially important first to know what the term "nation" means. The word is understood to refer to "a commonly shared circle of land, people and history surrounded by a periphery composed of all the other lands, peoples and histories." It is, in most cases, "inscribed within strict boundaries separating it from the rest of the world" (Herb and Kaplan 2008, 1364). As for nationalism, it implies drawing a line between "us" (insiders or fellow citizens) and "them" (outsiders).

Over the course of history, the world witnessed many deadly global and international wars for a number of centuries. From the An-Lushan Rebellion to the Mongol Conquest, Timur-e-Lang, the Qing Dynasty, the Napoleonic Wars, the Dungan Revolt, the Taiping Rebellion, the

Russian Civil War, World War I, and World War II, the world lost millions of lives. During these wars, nations exploited solidarity as a tool of nationalism to mobilize citizens to fight the wars of conquest, territorial expansion, hegemony, reform, autonomy, national interest, and self-determination.

The number of lives lost in these wars was an indication that humanity cares little about lives beyond their borders. Yet true citizens always value the lives of all human beings, including those beyond their international borders. Although there were numerous other wars in the past, the aforementioned top ten bloody wars in the history of the human race were fought in only two ages of civilization: they started during the age of agriculture and subsided at the height of the Industrial Age.

After the Second World War, the scope of nationalism was later expanded to allow for flexibility of choice. Unlike in the past, the period covering the ages of service, information, and communication has enabled citizens around the globe to understand the dangers of populism and extremism in fighting unnecessary wars. With the advancement of technology, the world has now become a global village in which no nation is an island. Information sent from one end of the globe is easily heard at the other end within an hour. This timely access to information has denied leaders who may mobilize citizens for unnecessary wars the leverage to do so, as their actions can be thwarted with ease by the world leaders and international organizations supervising world peace.

Over the last ten years, the Arab world and some African countries have been in turmoil from internal uprisings. The renowned Arab Spring which swarmed the Arab countries starting with Tunisia, Libya, Algeria, Egypt and Sudan, and currently Yemen and Syria, was a sign that the traditional ways of fostering nationalism have no place in the age of communication. The invention of Facebook, Twitter, WhatsApp, Instagram, and other social media platforms played an instrumental role in promoting a greater flow of information than ever before. Some citizens in these countries used social media negatively to incite violence rather than preaching peace and reconciliation, thus making it difficult to end civil wars.

While it is important to share information with the public, good citizens must always be cautious in disseminating information that inflict more harm on citizens rather than alleviating their suffering. Social media, in this sense, should be used as a platform where citizens preach peace and unity rather than hate and division.

Types of Nationalism

At the opening of this chapter, you might have gotten insight into what nationalism is all about and why we should embrace it. If that is the case, then it is now time for us to examine, discuss and compare the different types of nationalism that we will find below. Of course, there are many different types of nationalism, but for the purposes of this book, we will focus only on the six most relevant types: civic nationalism, cultural nationalism, ethnic nationalism, religious nationalism, racial nationalism, and diaspora nationalism.

In their book titled *Nations and Nationalism*, Guntram H. Herb and David H. Kaplan (2008) argue that "what distinguishes loyalty to a nation [from other forms of devotion] is the primacy it holds on people's allegiance" (xi). They were amazed by people's willingness to give their lives to ensure the continued existence of the group members and/or territories that make up their nations.

Such incredulity was also informed by past conflict patterns in which countries found themselves united when faced with an external threat or when their interest was affected. For instance, when Gavrilo Princip, a member of the Serbian-nationalist terrorist group popularly known as Black Hand in Sarajevo, assassinated the heir to the Austrian throne, Archduke Franz Ferdinand, on June 28, 1914, the whole world polarized along economic lines, sparking the deadly World War I. Alliances motivated by imperialism, militarism, and nationalism came into play with immediate effect as these countries fought a war that led to the loss of an estimated fifteen to nineteen million lives and about twenty-three million wounded military personnel, placing it among the deadliest conflicts in human history.

As you go through the types of nationalism discussed below, you may notice how they are interrelated, although in unusual ways.

Civic Nationalism

Also known as liberal nationalism, civic nationalism is identified by political philosophers who believe in an inclusive form of nationalism that adheres to traditional liberal values of freedom, tolerance, equality, and individual rights. In this sense, a civic nation need not be unified by commonalities of language or culture, where "culture" refers to the traditions and customs of a particular national group. It merely requires a disposition on the part of the nation's citizens to uphold their political institutions and to accept the liberal principles on which they are based. In this setting, membership is open to anyone who shares these values regardless of tribe, race, creed, or culture.

In a civic nation, the protection or promotion of one national culture over others is not a goal of the state, as it is considered biased. No religion, race, or culture is given special treatment. This type of nationalism is being practiced by countries such as France, Canada, and the United States that consider themselves to be relatively open societies and offer citizenship rights to all peoples regardless of their backgrounds.

Many scholars worked to make this form of nationalism a reality. There are several theories on the subject, but the most prominent theorist within the tradition of civic nationalism is John Stuart Mill, who once argued that it is "a necessary condition of free institutions that the boundaries of governments should coincide in the main with those of nationalities" — that is, that free institutions are next to impossible in a country made up of different nationalities.

Cultural Nationalism

Cultural nationalism refers to a type of nationalism where a nation sees itself through the lens of a shared culture. Sociologist Eric Taylor Woods (2015) defines it as "ideas and practices that relate to the intended revival of a purported national community's culture." This type of nationalism is an intermediate position between ethnic nationalism and civic nationalism, as it focuses on a national identity shaped by cultural traditions delinked from concepts of common ancestry or race.

Countries like China have preferred this form of nationalism to foster national unity. Prasenjit Duara, an Indian-American historian of China, argues that Chinese culturalism created a framework for a unified political community long before the Western concept of nationalism reached China in the nineteenth century. Duara defines Chinese culturalism as a mix between the Confucian high culturalism of the educated class and Han Chinese ethnic affiliation, viewing this as a factor enabling the people of China to imagine themselves as part of a unified community defined by culture.

There is a relationship between cultural nationalism and another less popular form known as political nationalism, which focuses on "the achievement of political autonomy." While political nationalism focuses on political independence, cultural nationalism, on the other hand, focuses on "the cultivation of a nation" and is driven primarily by intellectuals and artists. In this respect, "the vision of the government is not a political organization, but a moral community." As such, cultural nationalism is designed to give a roadmap to a country's "identity, history, and destiny" (Woods 2015).

Ethnic Nationalism

In ethnic nationalism or ethnonationalism, the state embraces ethnicity as its identity. This shared heritage is believed to include language, faith, and ethnic ancestry. Ethnic nationalists believe that the state should create a system that prioritizes the interest of a certain ethnic group over others. They believe strongly in a more monolithic state system of government rather than a diverse one that treats everybody as equal. They also argue that nationalism is inherited through ancestry, not granted to each individual upon the age of citizenship by their own merits.

Anyone who thinks that his own ethnic group is more qualified to be a nation of its own, while ignoring the presence and participation of other groups for whatever reason, falls under this category and qualifies as an ethnic nationalist. Good citizens should always take note of this type of nationalism and do everything possible to transcend it.

Religious Nationalism

Religious nationalism is the relationship of nationalism to a particular religious belief, dogma or affiliation. Such a link can be broken down into two aspects: the politicization of religion and the influence of religion on politics. Religious nationalism always harms the state's social fabric, as it discriminates against those whose religious ideologies are less recognized by the state. You cannot fully show pride in your nation if your religion is not being valued while another religion enjoys the full favor of the state.

There are countries where people with different faiths have found themselves further divided by their religious beliefs, such as Sri Lanka and the Sudan. For better understanding, I will focus on Sudan as the more familiar example.

To be precise, if you are South Sudanese, you were automatically a victim of religious nationalism in Sudan unless you were born after the independence of South Sudan in 2011. Despite the existence of Christianity in the north, the Sudanese government ruled the country for several decades with sharia law, Islamic religious law incorporated into the country's national constitution. Such law applied to all citizens, although the South Sudanese, who were mainly Christians, were against it.

Religious nationalism can be further divided into three subtypes: ethnic, ideological and ethno-ideological. Ethnic religious-nationalism comes about when people link religion and politics by employing religious identities for political ends. For instance, politicization of religion has created severe religious conflict between Catholics and Protestants in Ireland; Muslims in Chechnya and Tajikistan; Orthodox Serbs, Catholic Croats, and Muslim Bosnians in the former Yugoslavia; Tamil Hindus in Sri Lanka; and Muslims in Kashmir, among others.

Secondly, ideological religious nationalism religionizes politics by putting political issues and struggles within a sacred context, as seen in the Islamic revolution in Iran, Iraq and Syria. Liberation struggles influenced by ideological religious nationalism are always globalized, as seen in the Syrian civil war. The wars fought by Boko Haram, Al-Shabaab, ISIL, and Al-Qaeda are all religiously ideological, as they are aimed at establishing a world of Islamic States governed by sharia law.

The third approach, ethno-ideological religious nationalism, combines the first two and is both ethnic and ideological. The Israeli-Palestinian conflict exemplifies this last type. For decades, fundamentalists from both sides have directed this approach both against ideological foes from within their ethnic group and against their racial enemy.

Racial Nationalism

Racial nationalism refers to as an ideology that advocates for a racial definition of national identity. Proponents of racial nationalism believe that racial differences among people, such as skin color and other natural biological features, are the basis for social differences in human society and that these biological racial qualities determine people's material and spiritual life and all other social relations. Thus, people are divided into "superior" and "inferior" races.

This ideology is criticized the world over, with critics seeing it as a misleading application of the concept of nationalism. They argue that in reality, the notion of natural biological racial superiority and inferiority does not correctly reflect objective reality in human society. Critics of racial nationalism believe that racial differences are social phenomena rather than biological ones, revealing contradictions in the society's economic and class structures. For instance, during the era of slavery, the contradiction was between the slave-owning classes and the slaves themselves.

In countries where racism is high, the so-called superior race is considered the creator of material and spiritual civilization, destined to rule, while the inferior race is seen as sub-human and meant to be governed. Racial nationalism seeks to preserve a given race through policies such as banning race mixing and the immigration of other races, as in apartheid South Africa. With the recent rise to power of populists in Europe and the West, migrants are worried that the return of racial nationalism to the global stage is imminent.

Diaspora Nationalism

The word "diaspora" is an ancient Greek term that first appears in the Greek translation of the Hebrew Bible, the *Septuagint*, in the third century BC, "in which it described the divine punishment Jews would endure (i.e. their dispersion throughout the world) if they would not respect the law of God" (Herb and Kaplan 2008, 1366). Until the 1960s, the concept of diaspora was primarily applied to religious contexts, with a negative connotation of "exile and persecution." In addition to Jews, the term was also applied to Catholics and Protestants to label them as "religious minorities." However, since the 1960s, "new developments have occurred and the word has acquired a much more positive meaning without yet replacing the negative one" (Herb and Kaplan 2008, 1366).

Diaspora is the name normally used in political discourses for people living abroad. It has replaced the names formerly used, such as citizens abroad, nationals abroad, or populations living abroad, among others. However, it is much more inclusive than these former designations, as it maintains the idea that the nation is a family and that distance does not really matter as people used to think. Emotionally, it implies the opportunity to be in direct connection, more or less formally, with the homeland. Moreover, it also makes "diaspora policies" popular both inside and outside the country.

In the past, especially before the advancement of technology, people who left their territories for foreign countries were seen as lost citizens. In an article entitled "Mobilized and Proletarian Diasporas" (American Political Science Review, 1976), John Armstrong, one of the first scholars who scrutinized the role of diaspora, defined the term as "any ethnic collectivity that lacks a territorial base within a given polity." This connotes that they are a group living outside their country's boundaries.

Diaspora plays a fundamental role in any country's political development and progress. In 1996, a Burmese militant from the University of Wisconsin campaigned for democracy in Burma on his Free Burma Coalition site. As a result, the U.S. Congress imposed economic sanctions against the Rangoon regime.

In the case of South Sudan, the diaspora community has helped mobilize international support in many different ways. Writers, advocates (including artists such as Emmanuel Jal) and many more told the story of the South Sudanese and their plight across the Western countries. During the 2011 referendum, the South Sudanese living in diaspora were given an opportunity to vote in the plebiscite from special polling stations set up in eight countries with large South Sudanese populations: Australia, Canada, Egypt, Ethiopia, Kenya, Uganda, the United Kingdom, and the United States.

In the United States, where an estimated 25,000 to 50,000 South Sudanese resided at the time, polling booths were opened in the states of Virginia, Massachusetts, Illinois, Texas, Tennessee, Nebraska, Arizona, and Washington. Similar polling booths were also set up in the Canadian cities of Calgary and Toronto to cater for the South

Sudanese population there. Out of an estimated number of 40,000 to 50,000 Sudanese who lived in Canada, about 2,200 of them registered to vote in either of the two cities. In a nutshell, the diaspora community's campaign for the separation was an added asset to South Sudan's independence from the Sudan in the year 2011.

Transcending Ethnic Identity

After you have examined the different types of nationalism, I believe you are now in a position to know what kind of a nationalist you are. People may misjudge your true nationalism and refer to you as a civil nationalist, cultural nationalist, ethnic nationalist, religious nationalist, racial nationalist, or diaspora nationalist. However, they may be right or wrong depending on your behaviors, deeds, beliefs, or your current whereabouts. Additionally, circumstances may sometimes help identify the true nature of your nationalism.

In December 2013, South Sudan lapsed into a deadly civil war two years after it gained independence. This conflict was the biggest test of the country's quest for nationalism and social cohesion as a nascent nation. The conflict occurred at the time when the country was supposed to take one step ahead to catch up with the rest of the world in achieving social cohesion, development prospects, and economic prosperity. However, it instead took two steps backward, or even more, as the foundation it laid in the aftermath of the independence crumbled. Fixing the ruins and gluing together the fragmented social fabric and the weakened nationalism after the war became another struggle that requires collective effort from all citizens.

Transcending ethnic identity may be time consuming, but it's still attainable for people with a shared struggle for over a century. To win the war against tribalism, South Sudanese must see themselves as one people of one nation. The slogan "one people, one nation" has been a rallying cry for proponents of nationalism who feel that the South Sudanese are still lagging behind in attaining true nationalism.

"One people, one nation," as we have been signing, is not a bad slogan. However, we need to understand that it is a powerful phrase that can only be pronounced by a loving heart. Saying it is one thing, but making it truly meaningful is another. Because of its power, this phrase should not only end at the level of the lip; it should go deep down into our subconscious minds for it to become a reality.

In my understanding, "one nation, one people" means we have shattered our racial barriers, spanned our religious differences, and thawed our political divides in order to form a new national community and become one big tribe called South Sudan. We have no other choice than to do this because a nation's great solidarity is founded on the feeling of the sacrifices that people made in the past and present, and those that they are prepared to make in the future.

Nationalism is an important element in the nation-building process. It means that you love your nation and its inhabitants the same way you love yourself and your family. Nowadays, there is a growing sentiment that the nationalistic public rarely entertains government corruption, as they always advocate for change and reform. The recent strikes in Lebanon and Bolivia, where governments were forced to adopt reforms, speak volumes.

Another advantage of having nationalistic citizens is their respect for the rule of law. According to the World Bank's data on citizens' adherence to laws, countries endowed with higher levels of nationalism tend to have a stronger rule of law than those with a weak sense of nationalism. This is because their love and care for each other supersede their wish to harm one another.

As a citizen, you can either be a nationalist or a tribalist, since you cannot be both. While nationalism is an act of advancing the interest of the entire nation, tribalism, on the other hand, means that you are working for the sole interest of your tribe at the expense of others. This situation can be transformed too, and I am hopeful because many nations have passed this litmus test in the past. If, for example, you were more tribalistic last year, it is not difficult to do your country a favor by becoming less tribalistic this year and getting rid of the remaining elements of tribalism once and for all next year. I know it is possible if you decide to accept self-transformation. If you are capable of improving your level of understanding and upgrading your skills every year, you can also minimize your level of tribalism by upgrading your sense of nationalism.

This transformational process can also reduce the structural violence we sometimes experience in our nation, especially in the workplace. When I talk of structural violence, I mean cold wars such as those being waged at our workplaces by recruitment officers and managers. Sometimes as a manager, you may have your relatives serving in the same organization with you. If there is a vacancy that needs to be filled, you have to abide by the set criteria of hiring.

If your close relatives, such as nephews and cousins, are among the applicants, you need to be very careful in the choice you make to overcome the temptation of manipulating the organization's recruitment policy. As a human, you may sometimes need to empathize with your relatives and feel like disrupting the environment and hiring these immediate family members because you feel their plight more than those who are not related to you by blood.

However, the moment you try to alter the recruitment process and hire your relatives when they do not meet the set criteria, then you have already compromised your good citizenship traits and become a nepotistic boss. If you used to be regarded as a true nationalist prior to that, then you must now relinquish that identity — you no longer deserve it because you have lowered yourself into a nepotistic citizen, which is the lower tier of tribalism.

As citizens, we sometime succumb to our egos that encourage tribalism rather than nationalism. We fail to understand that God did not consult us when he created us in our present tribes. As such, if you know that you did not play any role in your being born a Shilluk, Nuer, Dinka, Bari, Murle or any other tribe, there is no reason for you to think that your ethnic group is better than other ethnic groups. We should not discriminate against others, because we would not be happy if we were discriminated against either.

Promoting Unity in Diversity

The term "unity in diversity" refers to the state of togetherness or oneness for people from different backgrounds. This concept is based on uniqueness and recognition. Proponents of the concept believe that individuals can be unique but should recognize their individual differences. These differences can include race, ethnicity, culture, gender, sexual orientation, socioeconomic status, age, physical abilities, religious beliefs, political beliefs, or other ideologies.

Unity in diversity is critical in any country because it facilitates the integration process for people with different views and ideologies. Whenever there is unity among the people despite their differences, it's always impossible for negative forces to disintegrate the nation.

Nationalism does not develop on its own, as one may think. It is a result of a group's unity, hidden in a purpose-oriented solidarity. During the war, our fathers were united in the fight for self-determination that gave birth to the independent South Sudan. In my childhood, I saw people speaking different languages in my hometown at a time when South Sudanese were so confined to their tribal enclaves.

My father, who was a member of Anya-Nya I and Anya-Nya II, as well as the SPLM/A, used to tell me stories of the armed movement and how good his friends and colleagues in the liberation struggle were, including how they coexisted peacefully even though they came from different regions and tribes. He knew that to achieve a cause more significant than what one could carry alone on his shoulder, it is not necessary to speak one language, have one culture, share one faith, or come from the same tribe. During his time, he understood that what matters is the cause itself and the group interest to achieve that cause than anything else.

Given this brief background, our fathers expected us to stay united and be peaceful to one another for us to be able to fulfill their wishes. However, there are a host of activities that are currently upsetting such aspirations and threaten our unity in diversity. Among the things I believe are angering our departed liberators is how we use the power we possess when we are entrusted with institutional leadership by the masses. Let's say, for example, you hold a position in an organization, company, or governmental institution, and you refuse to be guided by the institutional framework or policy; you are already letting down those who laid the national foundation of this country.

If you are a nepotistic boss who only employs or promotes his or her own relatives and friends at the expense of many qualified staff or long-serving civil servants in that institution whenever there is an opportunity or a vacancy available, you are not only demotivating your subordinates but also sowing the seeds of discord in that particular institution.

Such seeds will not only grow there; they will multiply, spread, and fill the country because the ones you are mistreating will copy your teaching and reciprocate it elsewhere once they get an opportunity to lead. Here, you will be remembered as an evil farmer who once planted bitter seeds that not only harmed his institution but also poisoned the entire nation with tribalism, discrimination, and nepotism. I hope that is not the legacy you would want to leave behind, as you can do more than that. You still stand a chance to correct yourself and become a good citizen who works as per the wishes of his progenitors, in which promotion of unity in diversity through a fair recruitment process is key.

Identifying the Unifying Factors

If anything has ever united South Sudanese under one umbrella as one people of one nation, one would proudly say it was the referendum for self-determination, which resulted in an independent South Sudan. At the time, the country had three active rebel movements: the South Sudan Liberation Army/Movement (SSLA/M), the South Sudan Democratic Army/Movement (SSDA/M), and the fiery Cobra Faction. On the day of voting, all of them silenced their guns to give room for the smooth conduct of the referendum.

The commanders also went to the media and assured the public about their decision to halt the fighting throughout the voting process. They adhered to their promise, and the referendum process went untampered until the end. Although they resumed the fighting in the immediate aftermath of the referendum, they had already shown that independence was a cause more significant than their private grievances.

Nationalism is an essential unifying factor in any country. Nations stay together when citizens communicate and share a good number of values and preferences. French historian Ernest Renan asserts that the critical conditions for being a people are to have common glories in the past, to have a collective will in the present, to have performed great deeds together, and to wish to perform still more.

South Sudan's historic liberation struggle against marginalization and political domination was also seen as the most important unifying factor, which fostered unity among the South Sudanese during the civil war. Veterans who fought the wars of independence would tell you that the reason they suffered at the hands of the successive regimes in the Sudan was because they were seen as one people, although they had various identities in the country's southern region.

Besides the shared struggles, we have a similar culture and tradition as South Sudanese, including our way of dressing. Christianity was conjointly our absolute faith as Southerners, when Northerners were mainly Muslim at the time. As for national language, Arabic was the official language of the Northerners, while we were using English as our official language in the SPLM/A liberated areas.

With independent South Sudan, most of these distinctions remained intact, with the exception of the Islamic religion, which had gained an increased number of followers as compared to during wartime, when it was confined to the capital Juba and a few other provincial capitals, where the faithful were mainly Sudanese traders and soldiers. Today, one would say that we have different religious groups, with Christianity being the dominant religion, followed by Islam and other faiths.

When we emphasize our unifying factors, it is good to avoid ranking them based on their importance, as that will only create a bitter atmosphere. If we say, for example, that we identify ourselves with Christianity, do you think other faith groups will be happy with this identity? I think not, because they would feel excluded. And if we see ourselves along tribal lines, we will not be fair enough to one another either. Moreover, if we all identified ourselves with one political party, the democratic principles of the multiparty system would die a permanent political death.

One may succumb to his ego and brag that his tribe is the best of all the tribes in the country. If we happen to possess such a habit of pride while clutching the banner of ethnic superiority instead of supporting the quest for national identity of oneness, then other people cannot see us as good citizens. Instead, they will see us as tribal lords and extremists.

Of course, as humans, we sometimes forget that our actions could hurt other people's feelings even when we say things that others could consider hurtful. A good citizen knows what is hurtful to his fellow countrymen and what is not. If we see ourselves through tribal lenses, our social fabric as a people could be weakened by tribalism itself, nepotism, discrimination, and at worst, by violent conflict.

Since we all know that these other identities can only divide us rather than bind us as one people, I think it would be wise if we can identify ourselves as South Sudanese. If we do this, then we can surely be under a single umbrella of one nation.

Negative Use of Nationalism

One of nature's laws, which has passed generational empirical tests, perhaps since the creation, is the law of excess. When anything is used excessively, a terrible ramification always follows. On every continent without exception, in this century alone, you have heard or are still hearing of xenophobic attacks, religious extremism, racial discrimination, tribal violence, and many more. All these are the baleful consequence of virulent nationalism, which has been taken to the extreme by those who still call themselves nationalists.

In a situation where nationalism is not counterbalanced by a moral doctrine that values self-control, or when it is used by citizens to impinge the rights of others, particularly the minority groups, and when it is diluted with tribalism, it always produces a catastrophic result.

One of the remarkable causes of mass violence that emanates from the detrimental use of nationalism is the exclusionary policy. Most of the civil wars that were fought in African countries, particularly during the post-independence era since the 1960s, were blamed primarily on exclusionary policies and tribal consciousness. For instance, the marginalization of and subsequent denial of job opportunities to the young people as practiced by the Sierra Leonean ruling elites sparked the civil war there, which ravaged the country for a period of eleven years. Such a policy also resembles the earlier form of nationalism in Europe, which was mainly linked to economic development and political segregation.

When regimes fail to manage civilians' grievances at the initial stage, they always manifest into uncontrollable chaos and civil disorder, which sometimes results in intra-state conflict or civil war. In times of crisis, populist politicians always emerge and exploit the situation to their political advantage. When an animalistic ego of an aggrieved citizen is kindled, it becomes challenging to reverse the situation to normalcy.

Another deadly menace of virulent nationalism is expansionism policy. When states tend to expand their territorial boundaries out of superiority, nations are always dragged into unnecessary interstate, regional, or even international wars. It is critical that good citizens desist from participating in activities that involve the negative use of nationalism.

ALLEGIANCE

*"Every man has a map in his heart of his own country
and the heart will never allow you to forget this map."*
Alexander McCall Smith

IN CHAPTER ONE, WE DISCUSSED THE IMPORTANCE of nationalism in its different forms. We also learned about the negative effects of nationalism when it is misused. However, in this chapter, we are going to discuss the importance of allegiance, including why it is obligatory for a good citizen to pay allegiance to his country and its flag. As you continue to read, you will find that the chapter is equipped with numerous case studies from other countries that show allegiance to be one of the important traits of good citizenship.

Allegiance, according to the Oxford Dictionary, means loyalty or commitment of a subordinate to a superior or of an individual to a group or cause. In this book, we will discuss it as a commitment to a cause.

In every country, the show of loyalty to one's nation is done through salutation of the flag and singing of the national anthem. In some instances, citizens use music to express their feelings for their flag and the ideals and values that it represents. One may want to know the meaning of the national anthem and why it is sung. To be precise, first of all, let me avoid universalizing the definition by contextualizing it in South Sudan.

As a South Sudanese myself, I understand of the national anthem as a remembrance of the soldiers who fought long and hard to liberate us. Not only that, it is an appreciation to God for the gift of a beautiful land blessed with various natural resources. Furthermore, I see it as a living promise to respect and uphold the diversity and unity of the nation and a commitment to fulfill the dream of the fallen heroes and heroines.

Jane Hampton Cook, the author of *America's Star-Spangled Story*, pointed out that "we stand for the flag today, not to please ourselves but to honor those who paid the ultimate sacrifice for our freedom … not to focus on what divides us but on what unites us … not for our generation but to set an example for the next generation." Cook also underscored that the American pledge of allegiance is not directed to the president, but to honor the reality that the United States has an elected president and not a lifetime king.

The idea of a pledge of allegiance is not something new to our world. In 1892, Francis Bellamy authored the American pledge of allegiance, which was originally recited with a palm-out gesture, the Bellamy salute, invented by James B. Upham. Bellamy's published instructions for the National School Celebration of Columbus Day also indicate that the salute was first demonstrated on October 12, 1892. In the published instructions, he recalled that Upham, upon reading the pledge, came into the posture of the salute, snapped his heels together, and said: "Now up there is the flag; I come to salute; as I say 'I pledge allegiance to my flag,' I stretch out my right hand and keep it raised while I say the stirring words that follow."

In the 1920s, Italian fascists adopted a similar gesture, which they branded as a "Roman salute" to symbolize that they had revitalized Italy on the model of ancient Rome. Nazi Germany also enacted a similar ritual in the 1930s. As a result, the United States replaced the Bellamy salute with the hand-over-heart tribute. Despite the counter-backlash from those who felt it was inappropriate for Americans to have to change the traditional salute because political movements in other countries had later adopted a similar gesture, the hand-over-heart tribute won over that of Bellamy.

As I mentioned above, the payment of allegiance is genuinely made in most cases by saluting the flying flag, whose colors have special meanings to us all as citizens who represent a broad spectrum of tribes, languages, creeds, cultures, and civilizations. If you have an image of your beautiful flag in your heart, as stated by Alexander McCall Smith, you will observe that South Sudan's flag has six different colors: red, white, yellow, green, blue, and black. All these beautiful colors that make up our amazing flag have different meanings.

Meaning of the Colors of South Sudan's Flag

Throughout the world, national flags are embraced and viewed by the citizens as symbols of national unity. South Sudan's flag, which is made up of black, red, blue, green, white and yellow, is no exception. Out of the six colors, black, red, and green are notably dominant. These three colors are separated by thin white stripes as they beautifully lie horizontally. On the hoist side of the flag, you will see that there is a blue triangular portion with a yellow star at the center.

To explain the meaning of the colors of South Sudan's flag, let me start with the red color. Red represents the blood of our martyrs spilled during the decades of liberation struggle for us to be free and become a dignified people in the republic today. We have to remember that if we are living comfortably and enjoying life today, it is because a certain brave, courageous, and selfless soldier, whom we will never see again and whose name we will not even know, took up arms and fought very hard in order to liberate us and set us free from the bondage of slavery, discrimination, and oppression. He did not enjoy the fruits of his struggle, he did not witness the fulfillment of his dream, and he does not know the fate of his children after his demise in the jungle of South Sudan. That brave soldier and good citizen does not need any expensive payback; all he needs is to see you enjoying those fruits of his sacrifice with your fellow South Sudanese from all tribes and creeds. He would be happy from heaven above if he sees that South Sudanese citizens embrace each other as one people.

Secondly, the two horizontal white stripes stand for the peace and unity of our nation. Throughout the liberation struggle, South Sudanese signed several peace pacts with the North, including the Addis Ababa peace agreement of 1972, the Khartoum peace agreement of 1997, and the Naivasha peace agreement of 2005 that ultimately brought an end to the decades-long civil war.

Let's see what the green color represents. This particular color signifies the beautiful land, agriculture, and natural resources we have in our amazing country today. I hope you know that our country is blessed with mineral resources such as oil, gold, and diamond, among others. Above all, we have a very fertile soil suitable for agriculture. Robert Mugabe once joked that Zimbabwe is so fertile to the extent that even a nail can germinate if planted. Although our soil cannot make a nail to germinate, it can germinate all types of crops we have in the world. Our soil is virgin, as a large part of it has never been exploited since the creation of Adam and Eve.

Most communities in South Sudan today are fighting over cattle, which only denies their children a right to education as we engage them in looking after cows. Instead of following cattle every day, can we consider producing our own food, eating from what we planted instead of depending on imported food, and giving our children a chance to study? We are strong people who are capable of working, except that we lack the spirit and appetite to do so. In many societies, it is considered shameful and insulting for a healthy and strong person to depend solely on food aid and imported products.

When you look at our national flag, there is another beautiful color, which is of great importance to us as a people. This color is blue, and it appears on the flag in the shape of a triangle. It stands for the Nile River and its water. One may wonder why we value the Nile River so much more than other communities of nations found along its banks. I would simply say that it's because the River Nile has been the source of life and survival for most South Sudanese for many centuries. Besides its clean water, it helped us in many different ways during the liberation struggle.

1988 saw the worst famine in the history of South Sudan. There was a failure of harvest across the land, as crops could not grow due to inconsistent rainfall, which was little at the start and became more excessive toward the end of the planting season. So many people died that year, as there was no food aid amidst the deadly civil war.

Many people tried to flee to neighboring countries for refuge, but a good number of them perished on the way as they painfully trekked to reach their unknown destinations. Some people decided to remain inside the country and persevered with the situation by all means, including by living inside the swamps of the River Nile. People ventured into the Nile for survival as it offered fish and other resources.

In addition, during the liberation struggle, the islands along the River Nile served as safe havens for the fleeing citizens. Whenever there was heavy bombardment or an attack, civilians would run and hide deep inside the Nile. Once there, you would be sure of your safety, since no enemy would dare to pursue you there, given the depth and thickness of its grass. The River Nile is also remembered because it is the longest river in the world, and we are blessed to have it crossing our country from the south to the far north. As such, it deserves recognition.

The yellow color on the flag, which is a star-like shape, represents the vision of our founding fathers. Before we were born, our fathers envisaged a country where its citizens would be free from marginalization, discrimination, and political domination. After they suffered such treatment from successive Sudanese regimes, they decided to fight so that we would not suffer like them in the future. This shows that they were selfless and loved us more than they loved themselves, choosing to die for us so that we could live a free and comfortable life. Most of these people died, but the fulfillment of their dream depends on us.

These heroes left us with a responsibility to uphold their dream by promoting equality, freedom, unity, and respect for diversity among ourselves. You have to remember that they took up arms with the belief that an independent South Sudan where citizens are free and equal was possible to attain. We must follow the star the same way as the three biblical wise men were guided by the bright star to the place where Jesus Christ was born.

Last but not least, the shiny black color we see on our flag represents our dominant black color as a people. This does not mean that we do not have other racial colors; some ethnic groups within the republic are of light brown color. Our brothers and sisters who are of light skin are sometimes viewed as foreigners by certain individuals from the dark-skinned race. This habit is discriminatory, and in some countries, it is punishable before the law. Individuals who are caught intentionally stereotyping their fellow citizens are always taken through corrective measures to discourage them from repeating the same.

It is incorrect to think that the country should possess only one racial color when it is inhabited by sixty-four tribes that are of Nilotic and Bantu origins. Despite our slight color difference, we are indivisible by our beliefs and dreams. After all, whether we identify ourselves as dark or light brown races, we should know that outsiders see us all as one people of black color.

Importance of Allegiance

At the Declaration of our Independence, one of the promises which every South Sudanese was happy about was the mention of equality and freedom as found in the bill of rights in our Constitution. This note was a promise that all men are born equal regardless of race, tribe, culture, or creed. The quest for freedom and equality is also what prompted Martin Luther King, Jr., to roll out his civil rights campaigns in the mid-twentieth century where he gave his "I Have a Dream" speech and demanded that both black and white men should be guaranteed the unalienable rights of life, liberty, and the pursuit of happiness.

The pledge of allegiance is a proclamation affirming that all citizens are unified, standing together as one nation and working together for the benefit of the country as a whole. It also means that the republic to which one belongs is under God, indivisible with liberty and justice for all. When we sing the national anthem and salute the flag, we are saluting the principle of justice enshrined in our constitution.

Every country in the world expects its citizens to pay unstinted allegiance to the nation at all times. Such allegiance is not paid to any specific entity, governmental institution, or political party, but to the nation as a whole. The national patriotic vow, which is often recited by citizens at formal governmental functions and public holidays, including Independence Day ceremonies, is a pledge of allegiance to the flag of the nation. The pledge of allegiance is also recited during the opening of Parliament, at most local-level government functions, and in schools.

One of the most interesting and touching national pledges is found in India. This famous national pledge recited by school children was composed in 1962 in Visakhapatnam, a city in Andhra Pradesh, by Pydimarri Venkata Subba Rao, who was then the district treasury officer. Subba Rao was a close associate of the nationalist leader Tenneti Viswanadham, who found the pledge interesting and forwarded it to the then Education Minister of Andhra Pradesh, Pusapati Vijayarama Gajapati Raju. Upon receipt, Raju directed all the schools in the district to have the students take the pledge. He also worked very hard to ensure that it was introduced at the national level.

In 1964, the Indian government's Advisory Committee for the Department of Education held a meeting in Bangalore in which they decided to introduce the pledge in all schools nationwide. In addition, the government translated it into seven languages and directed that it be recited in schools every day. Subba Rao only learned about its adoption as the National Pledge after his retirement, when he happened to hear his granddaughter read it from a school textbook.

One of the stanzas of this pledge says, "India is my country, and all Indians are my brothers and sisters." Today, Indians see themselves as inseparable because a good citizen in the person of Pydimarri Venkata Subba Rao united them through his well-written national pledge. If we, as citizens, all see ourselves as brothers and sisters, I believe violent conflict could be a thing of the past, as there would be no point in fighting one another.

Writing a national pledge is one thing; putting it into practice is another. From the above case, we have learned that school children have a pivotal role in publicizing national pledges everywhere. That is to say, for any national pledge to be widely known by the public, it has to be promoted by school children at all levels.

The reason why the pledge of allegiance is required to be recited daily in schools is that when a child recites the pledge every day, he or she may be directed into thinking more deeply about its meaning and significance. Daily recitation also instills a sense of patriotism among the children as they grow up loving their country. Unfortunately, most of those reciting the pledge today are saying it blindly as a ritual, as children and adults alike recite the words without actually internalizing them to understand their meaning.

In South Sudan, the national anthem is not widely recited, although it is a mark of patriotism to the country. It is an action that symbolizes one's loyalty to the republic and the feeling that, as a South Sudanese, one is proud to be a part of this beautiful and potentially prosperous nation with untapped golden opportunities.

In many countries, the pledge of allegiance is recited by schoolchildren of all religious backgrounds, including the atheists. Daily recitation is always done to honor the nation with more emphasis on her martyrs. In some countries, the recitation is not mandatory, since there are no punitive actions taken against those who do not recite the pledge. Sometimes, the Ministry of Education gives teachers strict instructions to ensure that the pledge of allegiance is taught and sung in all schools without exception.

In the United States, one of the cornerstones of an educational day is recitation of the national pledge of allegiance in schools. For many, it is one of the main tasks that is completed at the start of each day. The US pledge of allegiance reads, "I pledge allegiance to the Flag of the United States of America, and to the Republic for which it stands, one nation under God, indivisible, with liberty and justice for all."

There is a lot of debate regarding the recitation of the US pledge of allegiance. Many Americans don't say the pledge, as they feel that it's unnecessary even to stand up when the national anthem is being played. They defend their position saying that not reciting the pledge does not mean they are anti-patriotic. According to them, standing or not standing, reciting or not reciting, does not make one any more or less of an American citizen. However, it is expected that those who abstain from reciting the pledge should be seated quietly while the pledge is being said, thereby allowing the others to recite the pledge.

Furthermore, some people find the words "under God" in the American pledge of allegiance objectionable. For instance, atheists and non-Christian Americans argue that they cannot recite "under God" because it goes against their beliefs. Also, within the country, some believe that the refusal by some to say the pledge is a complete sign of disrespect to the country itself. This has left a controversy, as people with different schools of thought are debating and battling over the pledge and forgetting the larger objective of standing together in unity as a nation. Subsequently, the law has softened its stance on the reciting of the pledge, as each American has the freedom to choose to recite the pledge or not, so it is up to each individual.

It has to be remembered that the US Congress pushed for the addition of "under God" to the national pledge. One of Congress's reasons for adding "under God" to the pledge was to clarify America's disagreement with the Soviet Union regarding the character of human rights. The Soviets claimed that people receive their rights from the state, and therefore, the state can take those rights away. In contrast, Congress said it was using the phrase "under God" to make clear that basic human rights are beyond the reach of the state. So the Congress included the phrase "under God" to make a point and indirectly tell the Soviet Union to respect human rights.

In his inaugural address, President John F. Kennedy said, "The rights of man come not from the generosity of the State but from the Hand of God." Courts across the country acknowledge that the phrase "under God," rather than acting as a sort of prayer or spiritual creed, communicates timeless American values.

As for atheists, the phrase "under God" continued to be a thorn in their side. In June 2004, Dr. Michael Newdow, an atheist, filed a lawsuit with the US Supreme Court about the use of such phrases. The Supreme Court rejected the challenge, holding that Newdow did not have proper standing to challenge the pledge. His second attempt to challenge the pledge in March 2010 in California was likewise rebuffed by the Ninth Circuit Court of Appeals, which held "that the Pledge of Allegiance does not violate the Establishment Clause because Congress' ostensible and predominant purpose was to inspire patriotism." Refusing to give up, Newdow made a third attempt in New Hampshire in November 2010. This time, the First Circuit Court of Appeals rejected his claim because "both the choice to engage in the recitation of the pledge and the choice not to do so are entirely voluntary."

In Zimbabwe, the introduction of the national pledge in schools was met with an iron fist by certain politicians. Throughout the week in which it was introduced, numerous articles reported on the outcry by some politicians protesting its extension to Zimbabwe's schools. One of the opposition party officials, a lawyer, argued that the pledge was fascist and offered to take up the matter in the courts to challenge it. Despite this saga, Zimbabwe has a beautiful and touching national pledge today, which reads:

> "Almighty God in whose hands our future lies, I salute the national flag. United in our diversity, by our common desire for freedom, justice, and equality, respecting brave mothers and fathers who lost their lives in national liberation struggles, we are proud inheritors of our rich natural resources. We are proud creators and participants in our vibrant traditions and cultures. We commit to honesty and dignity of hard work."

Zimbabwe's national pledge has a lot of similarities with South Sudan's national anthem. In the pledge, they cite natural resources and emphasize the need to respect the perished heroes and heroines during the liberation struggle.

South Sudan's national unity is seen as a rather fragile concept. With this understanding, there is a better way to boost strong allegiance to the flag and a commitment to educate the next generation that a diverse South Sudan that they can all be proud of is still possible. Like the United States, India, Zimbabwe, and other countries I did not mention, South Sudan has one of the most beautiful national anthems ever created.

Before the independence, South Sudan's government constituted a committee to oversee the creation of a national anthem. During their tenure, the South Sudan National Anthem Committee received forty-nine entries for the national anthem from different composers. A competition was held live on South Sudan Television (SSTV), currently known as South Sudan Broadcasting Corporation (SSBC), in 2010 by artists of different calibers under the working title of "Land of Kush."

The competition was won by students and teachers of Juba University's Music Department, who composed an anthem titled "South Sudan Oyee." This preceded the referendum and the subsequent independence that led to South Sudan becoming a sovereign state. Although it was later amended to change the title and the tune, most words of the anthem remained the same. The latest version is as follows:

Oh God
We praise and glorify you
For Your grace on South Sudan,
The land of great abundance
Uphold us united in peace and harmony.
Oh motherland
We rise raising flag with the guiding star

And sing songs of freedom with joy;
For justice, liberty and prosperity
Shall forever more reign.
Oh great patriots
Let us stand up in silence and respect,
Saluting our martyrs whose blood
Cemented our national foundation,
We vow to protect our nation.
Oh God, bless South Sudan!

National Anthem and National Flag Code of Conduct

A national anthem, which can also be known as a state anthem, national hymn, or national song, is generally a patriotic musical composition that evokes and eulogizes the history, traditions, and struggles of its people, recognized either officially by a government or unofficially by the people. A national flag is a flag that represents and symbolizes a country.

Most countries have adopted laws that regulate the use of the national flag and the national anthem, given their importance. Some of these countries include China, Japan, German, Mexico, Thailand, and India. As we continue to examine the code of conduct in the aforementioned countries, let's begin our discussion with China.

The first flag-raising ceremony in China took place on Tiananmen Square in Beijing, the capital city, on October 1, 1949, during the Proclamation of the People's Republic of China. For the next two decades, the raising of the flag was done by electrical means except on the October 1 anniversary each year. From 1977 to 1982, the official ceremony involved soldiers from the People's Liberation Army raising the flag, after which the newly instituted People's Armed Police and its honor guard took over the performing of the ceremony for the next thirty-five years.

In 1990, the People's Republic of China adopted a law that they called the "Law of the People's Republic of China on the National Flag." Article 1 of this law required the citizens to defend the dignity of the national flag at all times. The same clause also spoke of enhancing citizens' consciousness of the State and promoting the spirit of patriotism. Article 3 of the law called on all citizens and organizations to respect and care for the national flag as the symbol and hallmark of the People's Republic of China.

In 2017, prior to the recent trade war between China and the United States, China drafted a bill that bans the placing of the palm over the heart. Chen Guoling, a member of the National People's Congress Standing Committee that was tasked with the drafting of the bill, explained why China decided to impose the ban:

> "Young people always put their right hands over their hearts under the national anthem, especially certain sports players. But it is not acceptable as this is an act originated from America in 1942. Americans do this to salute the US."

China's draft national anthem law states that when the anthem is heard, citizens should salute with their eyes, while members of the military on service duty should raise their hands in a salute. The draft law also indicated that any malicious revisions to the lyrics or derogatory performances in a public venue that damage the solemn image of the "March of the Volunteers," the national anthem of the People's Republic of China, are acts punishable with up to fifteen days' detention.

In Thailand, the national song is played every day on TV and in public places such as parks, schools, and offices at 8 am and 6 pm. Besides the national anthem, Thailand has a separate royal anthem called "Sansoen Phra Barami," which is played before every cinema screening, major musical performance, and sporting event. To date, the monarchy is still immensely revered in Thailand, and "disrespecting" the royal family carries a maximum jail term of fifteen years due to the country's harsh lèse-majesté laws. As with the national anthem,

Thais can be arrested for not standing while the royal anthem plays, although there is no official penalty for the act.

Citizens in most countries are required to stand as a mark of respect to the pledge. In the last decade, more than 400 teachers in Tokyo lost their jobs, with some being disciplined by their schools, for refusing to stand during the national anthem, which some see as too militaristic. Japan's national flag and anthem, "Kimigayo," and guidelines for their use were only established in 1999. The playing of the song and displaying of the flag were made mandatory in many Tokyo school ceremonies in 2004 by then-governor Shintaro Ishihara.

In India, the country's highest court once ruled that all cinemas must play the national anthem before a movie is played. Additionally, all audience members are required by the law to stand in respect of the national song. Under the Prevention of Insults to National Honour Act, people who intentionally prevent the singing of the anthem or cause any disturbance are liable for imprisonment for up to three years, a fine, or both.

Some countries impose penalties on citizens who do not comply with the code of conduct regulating the use of the national anthem. Citizens are sometime obligated to pay fines for failing to adhere to the national anthem code of conduct, including singing it incorrectly. In 2004, a woman in Mexico who got the words of the national anthem wrong before a soccer match was fined US$40.

Germany is one of the countries that have no national anthem law. However, it has strict rules that punish "defamation of the state and its symbols," including the anthem. The criminal code states, "whoever publicly insults the colors, flag, coat of arms or the anthem of the Federal Republic of Germany or one of its states shall be liable to imprisonment not exceeding three years or a fine." This rule calls for punishment of up to five years' imprisonment if the act was done intentionally to support "efforts against the continued existence" of the country or its "constitutional principles."

By having a national pledge, South Sudan is laying the groundwork to discipline and foster active participation of children in a context that, by and large, will put an end to the desire for armed conflict, including politics of individualism and tribalism. It can also strengthen the realization that through collective responsibility, this country can achieve greater heights.

THREE

ADHERENCE TO RULE OF LAW

"When freedom does not have a purpose, when it does not wish to know anything about the rule of law engraved in the hearts of men and women, when it does not listen to the voice of conscience, it turns against humanity and society."
Pope John Paul II

IN CHAPTER TWO, WE DISCUSSED THE IMPORTANCE of allegiance, including a number of case studies from the developed states, particularly the United States, China, and some European countries. We also talked about the code of conduct for the national anthem and the flag. In this chapter, we will discuss adherence to the rule of law, with a specific focus on the importance of law, the benefits of obedience to the law, policing and human rights, and community policing.

To begin with, let's first define the term "law." Law is defined as a system of rules and guidelines, which are enforced through social institutions to govern behaviors. Thousands of years ago, we used to live in a state of nature. At that time, we lived an "eat me if you find me" or "I will eat you if I find you" kind of life. Life was hard because humans were living and behaving like wild animals in the jungle. Everyone was both predator and prey, as you would do away with those who are weaker than you, while those who are stronger than you would do away with you. To protect the vulnerable from the notorious strong, people saw it as a good idea to make laws that could regulate such harmful behaviors.

In Africa, laws are historically closely linked to the development of civilization, such as that of Ancient Egypt, which dates back as far as 3000 BC. That system contained a civil code that was broken into twelve books based on the concept of justice or ma'at and characterized by tradition, rhetorical speech, social equality, and impartiality. The introduction of the law was a great achievement on the African continent, as it saved humanity from the brutality of many who used the state of lawlessness to advance their goals.

Another great achievement in the past thousand years was the introduction of law and order on the European continent. In the twelfth century, the Europeans started the systemic application of law and order, marking the turning point in their continent's history. Law books were compiled and jurisprudence was developed. In the same century, England also developed its justice system and established a trial jury.

In Asia, the Babylonians served as flagship in the application of law. In the twenty-second century BC, the ancient Sumerian (modern-day southern Iraq) ruler Ur-Nammu formulated the first law code, which consisted of if/then statements: if you violate the law, then you will be punished accordingly. By around 1760 BC, King Hammurabi further developed Babylonian law by codifying and inscribing it in stone. Hammurabi placed several copies of his law code throughout the kingdom of Babylon as stone slabs or stelae for the entire public to see.

While the law is useful in protecting us from the negative behaviors of a few, they cannot work without the support of the citizens. In today's world, the ultimate gatekeepers of justice are informed citizens who monitor what is said, heard, seen, and even smelled. That is the essence of having ears, eyes, and mouths. The biblical prophets of ancient times are gone, leaving every single one of us to take their place in safeguarding justice. You have to understand that even the best of governments can fail if we do not attune our senses to catch the tell-tale signs of moral rot right in our backyard.

Every citizen must lend a hand of cooperation to law enforcement officials in the discharge of their duties. As citizens, we must respect the rules because they are clearly communicated and fairly enforced. Everyone is held responsible by the same laws, and those laws safeguard our vital rights. We should collectively try to remove evils and crimes from our society by rendering help to the police and justice agents.

Importance of Law

Law serves many purposes and functions in our society, as its principal goals and services are to establish standards, maintain order, resolve disputes, and protect liberties and rights. Law is seen as a guidepost for minimally acceptable behavior in the community. This is the reason why we also define the Constitution as a power map, deriving its whole authority from the governed. The Constitution regulates the allocation of powers, functions, and duties among the various agencies and organs of government and defines their relationship with the citizenry. Without it, our security and rights could be threatened.

The institutions of the country can survive for generations if the press, the schools, and the church can educate the great masses of the people up to a capacity for right thinking and judging on public matters. This, in my opinion, is the only hope that I think is sufficient.

I believe that God has laid the foundation of our republic, instincts, and character of the human race, as most of the divine laws revealed to prophets and apostles have been adapted into our Constitution. However, we cannot see real progress in bringing men into conformity with moral law if our quest to promote conformity with political law is faced with challenges.

While kings are chosen by the people to serve the people, legislatures are voted in by the people to serve them, priesthoods depend on the support of the people they serve, and a judiciary cannot serve justice without police power and the general public's support. Citizens thus have an inherent obligation to adhere to the rule of law.

Benefits of Obedience to the Law

The key benefit of obeying the laws and commands of the land is that they ensure people's happiness and wellbeing better than other alternatives. If a person fails to obey the law, other people in the society can also be affected negatively by his behavior and action. All citizens are expected not only to abide by the rule of law but also to take the responsibility to educate others to willingly and habitually obey the laws of the state. Good laws always reflect the will of the citizens, and as such, there shouldn't be any hesitation in obeying them.

In this highly charged political world, the implementation of law and order is very challenging as it faces resistance from different quarters of society. This is true whenever there is a full-fledged political instability. During the South Sudanese civil war, for instance, the country experienced terrible insecurity, which also affected the capital, Juba. As in any other country undergoing an active civil war, some civilians, both criminals and normal citizens alike, got access to firearms.

While normal citizens with access to arms used their weapons for self-defense, others decided to exploit the prevailing insecurity to terrorize the innocent majority. A term was coined to classify this group, "unknown gunmen," since it was difficult to identify them.

The reign of unknown gunmen was so horrific in the republic throughout the war years. Some citizens who felt insecure enough left the capital city either for sub-national levels or for refuge in the neighboring countries. Suburb areas were almost deserted, as those who were financially well-off preferred to live in hotels situated in the heart of the city instead of in their homes. This happened because some citizens decided to defy the rule of law and order in the wake of the economic crisis associated with the civil war.

In many countries, supporters of law and order, especially those from the right wing, always see incarceration as the most effective means of crime prevention. On the other hand, opponents of law and order, who are in most cases typically left-wing, believe that a system of harsh criminal punishment is ultimately ineffective because it does not tackle fundamental or general causes of crime. This gives critics of law-and-order politics a window to point to potential abuses of judicial and police powers, which in this case includes police brutality, misconduct, tribal profiling, prison overcrowding, and miscarriages of justice.

The existence of law and order is of paramount importance. No one is prepared to risk visiting a volatile country full of crimes and insecurity in this world. For example, if you want to travel to a place, the first question that comes into your mind is how safe that country is. You also have to remember that when conflict erupted in South Sudan, most investors who had businesses in the country halted their operations and fled for their safety, which struck a blow to our economy as they employed some of our fellow brothers and sisters in their companies. This means that if we choose to cause insecurity for whatever reason, we will automatically chase away these investors and make our people jobless. Once they are jobless, we will have an increased number of unknown gunmen on a daily basis.

I believe no one has the intention of creating instability and promoting crimes in the republic. As good citizens, we also have a responsibility to respect the authority figures who are directly compelling obedience and respect for law and order. If we honor the law, there is no reason why we cannot also honor those who directly implement it. There are many benefits to respecting the law.

In 2006, when I was still a college student, I was living in Kenya's capital city of Nairobi. One Saturday afternoon, I paid a visit to Nairobi town even though I didn't have a class that day. As energetic youth, we used to have a place in the heart of the city where we would idly sit and kill time, especially on weekends. In this place, we could discuss a range of issues, including school life, implementation of the comprehensive agreement, and referendum. Of course, 2006 was a wonderful year, coming right after the historical year 2005. I hope you know that 2005 is the year in which the Comprehensive Peace Agreement that gave birth to independent South Sudan was signed. Fresh memories of Dr. John Garang's historical speeches and the exciting masses who attended the signing ceremony of the CPA were still in our minds.

The conversations were so exhilarating, and I can attest that nothing is of interest like political discussion, especially when you are in your twenties. At that time, phones were not as numerous as they are today. As such, when one would get information pertaining to South Sudan, he would rush to the town where we all socialized and share it with the rest of the group members. Even a small piece of information is very important, as it can be broken into pieces and discussed for a whole week or even a month if nothing new is received.

Unfortunately, this time around, the Nairobi City Council was fed up with idle squatters in the heart of the town. The security and cleanliness of the city mattered a lot — the era of idle wanderers had to come to an end. Yes, we were discussing important national issues. But did they know what we were discussing? And if they knew it, did it concern them? None of these questions is important.

After all, it is not about Kenya; it is about an unborn country, still in the form of a dream. It may be liberated democratically through referendum polls, or it may not, if the citizens decide to vote for unity of the country. From another angle, perhaps they expected us to sit inside the hotels or restaurants and add value to the country's economy. But as students, we were struggling just to pay our school fees, not expensive beer and food.

As we were sitting on a horizontal metallic pole situated between two narrow roads, we were surprised by the Nairobi City Council (NCC) agents equipped with handcuffs and other crime-deterrent devices. They came in a big group and overwhelmed us. In less than a minute, I was already flanked by two giant guys who were about to pull me toward their pick-up vehicle parked by the roadside.

I don't want to brag here, but this is what happened. As a law-abiding person, I told them that I was not there to wrestle with law enforcement agents. I asked them if I could walk into the vehicle myself instead of being pulled. At first, they were reluctant, as they thought it was a trick for me to run. After a thoughtful moment, they accepted my plea. As I was voluntarily moving toward the vehicle, the head of the operation overheard my polite appeal, which to him signified respect for the rule of law and order. He told his men to set me free, saying, "The young man is a law-abiding person who deserves to be forgiven." I was set free, and I immediately headed home.

The other young men who were with me tried to resist the councilors' order. They were all rounded up, handcuffed, forced into the small pick-up vehicle, and taken into police custody. Some were badly injured in the course of resistance. These fellow South Sudanese were about twenty years old, and they had to fit inside a small pick-up vehicle simply because their egos told them to defy law and order. I never dared to go and sit in that place again until I completed my studies, since it was considered a breach of the city's laws.

The moral lesson of this story is that as a citizen, you need to respect civil servants tasked with the enforcement of law. A law implementer is a public servant who deserves respect just like you. You have to respect them so long as you respect the law. The power to compel obedience to the law is derived from the power to sway public opinion to the belief that the law and its agents are legitimate. In any normal situation, law and order are legitimate, and as such, people must respect them.

It may be difficult sometimes for people to follow the rule of law. However, the laws are made so that people do not get hurt physically or even with words. At the family level, parents may make rules to ensure that children and other family members are safe from dangerous people or risky places. For their part, police officers look out to make sure people do not break the rule of laws that safeguard the community. It is not because they like to find bad people; it is because they want to make sure others do not get hurt.

At school, teachers and education masters want students to abide by the rules and regulations. If there weren't any rules at school, it could be difficult for anyone to get the education they have a right to. As a good citizen, you must not attempt to defy a police officer's instruction or abuse him. He is not your enemy nor the one who made the law. He is just there to implement something that has been agreed upon by all citizens, including your representative in the parliament, if not you.

Policing and Human Rights

The police force always finds it challenging to strike a balance between controlling crime and protecting human rights. In a situation where rules that guide the dealings with the general public are fluid or unclear, citizens end up becoming victims of police brutality. In 2018, for instance, Venezuela topped the list of countries where police brutality was prevalent, as 5,287 people were killed in a period of one year by the security forces. Syria came second, with 4,162 people being killed by the security forces in the same year.

In the past, police brutality was an issue of great concern. Law enforcement agencies hardly treated suspects with respect as demanded by the law. Whenever the police apprehended a suspect, they would always see him as a criminal. As such, they would subject him to the harsh treatment that a criminal deserves. This is against the principles of policing, which require the police to treat a suspect with dignity and respect until he is proven guilty by the law.

This brutality forced the United Nations General Assembly to adopt a Code of Conduct for Law Enforcement that guides police in their operation across the world on December 17, 1979. The purpose of this code of conduct was to protect human rights as well as to assure equal treatment of citizens without discrimination. In any country, the police qualifies to be termed as an ideal police force only when it demonstrates democratic policing. This can be measured through essential characteristics such as accountability to citizens rather than to government.

Such accountability mechanisms should also create incentives for police to protect human rights, especially civil and political rights, as a hallmark of democracy. On the other hand, police accountability should incentivize them to give top operational priority to servicing the needs of individual citizens and private groups. Such security needs can best be addressed when police forces choose to be responsive rather than preventive. There should be accountability mechanisms that provide checks and balances on police action, sanctioning human rights violations and other violations of rules governing police behavior in the society.

Democratic policing is relevant not only for countries in transition but also for stable countries. A politicized police force, in many developing countries, has historically acted against citizens, as they are sometimes used as a tool by the ruling party, an authoritarian government, or a colonizing government. For instance, in Latin America, this legacy has produced a misconception of the role of the police, as citizens could not buy into the simple idea that the police are no enemy and that they are citizens too, as are those with whom they work.

Many police officers who did not go through proper orientation and training are either unaware of or do not see the importance of a law enforcement code of ethics. Within an agency's code of ethics, there are specific provisions that promote the safeguarding of lives and property, the importance of avoiding bias, as well as the understanding that the badge that they wear is a symbol of the public trust. Additionally, the code of ethics requires that officers are prepared not only to enforce the law but also to follow it.

Most law enforcement agencies have detailed and clearly written security policies that guide their operation. However, a security policy is of no use if it cannot be implemented in letter and spirit by the organization and the individuals working in that organization. For it to be effective, there must be a specific auditing process put in place to verify compliance with the framework. There must also be punitive actions to be taken in the event of non-compliance with the policy.

Community Policing

Community security, which is sometimes known as community safety, refers to the approach to implementing human security, human development, and state-building concepts at the local level. According to the United Nations Development Program (UNDP), it is understood as a concept that seeks to operationalize human security, human development, and state-building paradigms at the local level.

In the United Kingdom, when Sir Robert Peel, popularly known as "the Father of Community Security," established the London Metropolitan Police in 1829, he set forth several principles. One of these principles, which in the modern days is considered the seed of community policing, is his famous phrase that "the police are the public and the public are the police." This phrase only exists on paper nowadays, as the police and the public have become so separated from one another. In some communities today, an attitude of "us versus them" is what prevails between the police and the public.

For it to be effective, community policing requires the active participation of the local community, local authorities, civil society organizations, the business community, private agencies, residents, churches, schools, and hospitals, since it does not just refer to individual community members but to all actors, groups, and institutions within the specific geographic space.

In a nutshell, all who share a concern for the welfare of the neighborhood should bear responsibility for safeguarding such welfare in order to deliver security and other services in that area. Good citizens are each other's keepers. They share information about their safety and security that in turn helps the law enforcement agencies to protect them.

FOUR

PAYMENT OF TAXES

"Taxation is the price which civilized communities pay
for the opportunity of remaining civilized."
Albert Bushnell Hart

Now that you have learned about the adherence to the rule of law, its importance and benefits, policing, and human rights in the preceding chapter, it is now time to discuss payment of taxes, one of the important topics in this book. For you as a citizen, it is critical to know the different types of taxes and why they exist. Before we do that, let's first define the term "tax" and know where and how it originated.

Tax is a required contribution to the state revenue. In most countries, if not all, government levy tax on workers' income, financial gains, and business profits. Sometimes, it is added to the cost of certain goods, services, and transactions. In payment of tax, citizens are always concerned about what the government does with the money collected from them.

US President Calvin Coolidge argued that raising more taxes than necessary is like legalized robbery. I would say the collection of tax is not a bad idea, so long as citizens don't pay nearly half of everything they earn to the government. Moreover, taxation will continue to be useful so long as citizens see what their taxes are being used for. US President Barack Obama once underscored that people want fairness while paying their fair share of taxes.

Looking back through history, we see that taxation is not a new phenomenon for our nation or for the entire modern world. It existed even before biblical times, particularly in the Middle East, where the first accounting system used tokens that represented certain amounts of goods: for instance, two clay balls would represent two measures of grain. However, that system was no longer sufficient after the first state rose in Sumer around 3100 BC; the new political system asked citizens to contribute goods to the temple to be stored and redistributed.

In ancient Egypt, more than a millennium later, the book of Genesis records that Joseph established a law in which a fifth of the produce was to be given to Pharaoh. In Genesis, we are told that when the country accelerated its production to prepare for the seven-year famine, the surpluses were too big to measure, affirming that the government was well prepared to face the crisis.

As a nation in the aftermath of the Exodus, Israel levied a 10 percent tax on produce and herds. Because the tax was not used for general social welfare, but only to support the tabernacle and the priests, the tax rate was lower than in Egypt. Instead of using tax revenue to help the poor, Israel implemented regulations. For instance, the book of Leviticus calls for farmers to leave enough at the edges of their fields after the harvest for the "poor and the alien" to glean what they needed.

Also, it has to be noted that when Israel acquired a status of nationhood, its demands were greater than ever before. To bridge the economic gap brought about by rapid population growth, King Solomon decided to conscript about 30,000 men from across Israel to work as loggers in Lebanon, as written in the book of I Kings in the Old Testament. In the same vein, the nation instituted a poll tax and an income tax paid in provisions such as flour, meal, cattle, sheep, or fowl. However, such heavy taxation was a contributing factor in the division of the kingdom into Israel and Judea in 880 BC.

Today, all countries in the world are operating with revenues and taxes generated from natural resources, human resources, and social services. According to South Sudan's Constitution, our country is run with revenues generated from natural resources of mainly oil, transportation (air, land, and river), service charges, loans, national government enterprise projects, grant-in-aid, foreign financial assistance, fees from nationality documents (nationality and passport), immigration, royalties, and excise duties. To complement these revenues, we also collect a variety of taxes, such as personal income tax, corporate and business tax, customs duties and import tax, value-added tax, and capital gains tax.

Types of Taxes

There are multiple types of taxes in every country levied by different levels of government. In our country, different tiers of government collect different and sometimes similar types of taxes. For instance, some of the taxes collected at the national level are also levied at the state level. The county level seems to have less commonality in taxes with the two upper tiers of government. While in the global context, there are numerous types of taxes, as indicated above, for the purposes of this chapter, I will only focus on the types of taxes we have here in South Sudan.

If you go through our constitution — the Constitution of the Republic of South Sudan 2011 — you will find that chapter IV talks about sources of revenue for the national government. In that chapter, you will see that petroleum tops the list of resources we generate for our country's economy. In addition, Section 74 of our Local Government Act 2009 also focuses on the sources of revenue at the county level. These taxes include council property tax, social service tax, council land tax, animal tax, council sale tax, capital gains tax, produce tax, and many more. Without wasting your time, let's take a look at the different types of taxes we have in our country, especially at the national level.

Income Tax

An income tax is a type of charge that governments impose on income generated by both individuals and businesses within their jurisdiction. In short, it is levied on the money you earn or the business you do. These taxes are then used to fund public services, pay government obligations, and provide goods for citizens.

Income taxes are both progressive and marginal. We say an income tax is progressive because it imposes a lower tax rate on low-income earners compared to those with a higher income. This means the government has a show of sympathy to those earning less, as the payment is made based on the taxpayer's ability to pay. The income tax is therefore marginal because there are different tax rates for different income brackets. In this system, the top earners pay a higher tax rate than the low earners.

One thing that we need to take note of is that only the amount of money a person has in that top bracket is charged at the top rate. As such, if you read that someone is being taxed at the 35.4 percent rate, it's not their entire income multiplied by 0.354 that they end up paying.

Value Added Tax

Value added tax (VAT) or ad valorem is a type of tax charged on the "added value" of a product. It's a form of consumption tax that buyers pay when they make a purchase, similar to a sales tax. It shows the difference between the sales price and the cost of producing a good or service. You may need to know the difference between sales tax and VAT.

While the purchaser of a product pays sales tax, VAT, in contrast, is applied at each stage of the supply chain and then rolled into the final purchase price. If you travel to a country with VAT, you probably won't notice you're paying it because it will be included in the prices you pay. Sales tax, on the other hand, is listed separately on receipts.

In the sales tax, only that final stage in the product's life is subject to taxation.

Entrepreneurs need to know the VAT regulations for the countries in which they do business. In the Netherlands, for instance, after you have registered your business with the Chamber of Commerce, the Dutch Tax and Customs Administration will assess if you are an entrepreneur for VAT purposes. If you provide all of the details required by the Dutch Tax and Customs Administration when you register with the Dutch Commercial Register, they will provide you with a VAT number immediately. After that, you will be required to indicate your VAT number on all of your invoices. This practice is usually the case if you operate a company or work for yourself as a self-employed professional or freelancer. Because the conditions for VAT are different from those for income tax, it could be that you are considered an entrepreneur for VAT, but not for income tax purposes.

In some countries, foreign governments refund visitors who pay value added tax. A visitor may pay VAT while making purchases, but he can be refunded at the airport when he is about to leave the country, so long as he has the receipts. After that, visitors have a number of choices: they can buy souvenirs from a duty-free shop, exchange the foreign currency, or go home with the money.

While many visitors consider this policy of refunding superb, it also has its shortfalls. Let me use my own experience to support this argument. In autumn 2013, I paid a visit to Durban, South Africa. When I was about to leave the city, I went to the market to buy some souvenirs. Since South Africa practices value added tax, I was obliged to pay my VAT on those purchases. After that, I took a domestic flight from Durban to Johannesburg in order to take a connecting flight to my country.

Since I left late, I also arrived late, reaching Johannesburg around midnight. Before I could check in, I ventured into the office where the government refunds non-South African tourists who made purchases subject to VAT in South Africa. To my surprise, I was told the office was closed since it was midnight. As a result, I repacked my receipts and traveled home with them as souvenirs. Although the refund policy is good, it is of no meaning for anyone who is a late-night traveler.

Corporate and Business Profit Taxes

A corporate tax or business tax, which is also known as a corporation tax, is a direct tax imposed by an authority on the income or capital of corporations or analogous legal entities. Many countries in the world impose such taxes at the national level, and some also impose it on both federal and state levels.

In South Sudan, this type of tax is only found at the national level, as the Interim Transitional Constitution of the Republic of South Sudan 2011 waived states from paying it. When corporate tax is paid, you will allocate the payment to the "Provision for corporate tax" liability account, so the balance comes to zero.

In some jurisdictions, tax paid by a property owner is not considered a trade expense, but a private one, so it does not appear in the books of the business. Small businesses of all types may pay an estimated average effective tax rate of less than 20 percent. In this regard, the effective tax rate is the average rate of tax for a business or an individual taxpayer.

Property Tax

Property tax is a tax paid on homes, land, or commercial real estate. For instance, if you are deciding whether you can afford to buy a home, you should take property taxes into account. The money that the government generates through this tax is used for the development of local amenities such as repairing of the roads, construction of schools, sanitation, and buildings, among others.

In India, when the government wants to apply this tax, the municipal corporation of a particular area carries out an assessment and then imposes the property tax, which in most cases is paid annually or semi-annually. Usually, the tax amount is based on the area, construction, property size, building, and other factors. However, central government properties and vacant property are generally exempted from property tax payment since they are public institutions. The good thing about this type of tax is the flexibility exercised by the authorities dealing with it when it comes to payment. In many countries, you can choose to pay your property tax on an annual or half-yearly basis as per your comfort. This type of tax is mandatory in most first-world countries.

Unlike a mortgage, property tax payment does not amortize. Unless you qualify for property tax exemptions for seniors, veterans, or disabled residents, you have to keep paying them as long as you live in a home. Remember, property tax also comprises taxes such as lighting tax, water tax, and drainage tax.

Capital Gains Tax

A capital gain is a rise in the price of a capital asset — either investment or real estate — that offers it a better price than the acquisition was worth. An investor does not have a capital gain until an investment is sold for a profit. When you sell your venture and get a benefit, this is where the government will come in and tax your gain.

In more simple terms, capital gains taxes are taxes charged on investment income after the property is sold and a capital gain is realized. In other words, it is considered as levy assessed on the positive difference between the sale price of the asset and its original purchase price.

Long-term capital gains tax may be a levy on the profits from the sale of assets command for over a year. In South Sudan, many people do not invest, and as such, they don't pay capital gains tax.

Customs Duties and Import Taxes

Customs duty, also known as import tax, is a tariff or tax imposed on goods transported across international borders. The sole purpose of this type of charge is to protect each country's economy, residents, jobs, and environment, among others, by controlling the flow of goods, especially restrictive and prohibited goods, into and out of the country. The amount of tax you must pay depends on the type of products you carry. As such, countries have adopted something called customs valuation.

Customs valuation is the determination of the economic value of goods declared for importation. For the sake of efficiency, countries should choose a standard set of rules for establishing the value of these goods. Having a commonly agreed and accurate measuring standard is vital for economic and commercial policy analysis, application of industrial policy measures, proper collection of import duties and taxes, and import and export statistics. Customs duties and VAT are calculated as a percentage of the goods' value.

The value of imported goods is one of the three elements of taxation that provides the basis for the assessment of any customs debt (the technical term for the amount of duty that has to be paid after such an evaluation). As a general policy, customs duty can only be calculated once the value of goods has been determined.

Excise Duty

Excise duty is a form of indirect tax that is levied by the government on goods that have been manufactured in the country. It ideally needs to be paid by the manufacturer of products at the time of the introduction of those products into the market.

Excise duty is the opposite of customs duty. Both excise and customs duty are taxes levied by the government, but the significant difference between the two is that excise duty is the tax collected by the government on the products made within the country, whereas custom duty may be a tax levied upon goods imported from foreign countries.

On the other hand, excise duty and sales tax have slight similarities. While excise duty is on the production of goods, sales tax is levied on the sale of goods. It is also essential to know that excise duty is paid by the manufacturer, while the burden of sales tax is borne entirely by the end consumer. Additionally, excise duty is levied on accessible value, whereas sales tax is based on the sale price.

Why We Should Pay Tax

As I stated earlier, taxes are levied in almost every country in the world, primarily to raise revenue for government expenditures, although they sometimes serve other purposes. In modern economies, taxes are the most critical source of national income, especially in countries that lack mineral resources. They are also used to fund public facilities such as health care centers, education institutions, police stations, recreation facilities, and places of worship.

Payment of taxes is compulsory in both developed and developing countries. It is not about giving Caesar what belongs to Caesar; it is about giving the state what it deserves for its development and sustainability.

In all the years I have lived, I have never heard of a nation that is an example of development, yet does not levy tax from her citizens. Taxes can greatly boost the economies of countries that have no mineral resources. For instance, Switzerland, one such country that lacks natural resources, is run mainly with taxes, although it has other revenue sources. The administration of any country involves a certain amount of expenditure, and these expenditures cannot be met without raising certain taxes.

Taxes also facilitate the payment of workers for certain types of jobs. In some instances, the salary we receive comes partly from the tax we pay. For example, if you are a civil servant, you are already paying income tax. Therefore, for us to have a continued payment for our work, we have to comply with the rules regulating the payment of tax.

Some of us, including a few businesspersons, do not understand why they should pay tax. Others do not even see the critical role played by the police in providing security and enforcing law. This reminds me of the story in which one appreciates the importance of fresh air only when he is first locked up in a hot container for a few minutes before being released.

Let's say, for example, you are a businessperson who runs a restaurant in town. You will have to understand that your business is safe and booming because there are law agents who provide security for it to run. You may not see them physically, as they may not be deployed around your restaurant, but their presence through patrolling scares away the criminals who might loot your business. If you think it is not the police that provides security for your business, try to open it in the bush for only one day and see what will happen.

Now that you know that there are people who provide protection to you and to your properties, who else do you think should pay them? I know you will say the government. You need to understand that the government is just a system constituted by civil servants to administer the country and manage its operations. They don't have the money themselves; they run it through the taxes you pay. Therefore, it is in our interest as citizens to willingly and honestly make payment of these taxes so that our country is run smoothly by the government.

I know there are many concerns about the collection and management of taxes. The growing concern that taxes are misused when levied may be genuine. However, it is better to collect tax and mismanage it than to completely desist from its collection due to mismanagement. History tells us that any country that has just emerged from a civil war always struggles to make its institutions strong. It always takes time to have active civil servants capable of managing the country's resources for the welfare of all.

However, this should not be used to justify financial malpractice related to the management of taxes, because even in the Constitution, it is said that ignorance of the law should not be used as an excuse to violate the law. As such, the lack of financial management skills should not be a justification for tax mismanagement.

FIVE

PUBLIC SPIRIT AND VOLUNTEERING

*"The cock that crows in the morning belongs to one household
but his voice is the property of the neighborhood."*
Chinua Achebe

In CHAPTER FOUR, YOU READ ABOUT and hopefully understood why it is important for citizens to pay taxes. You also now know the origin of tax and its different types. In this chapter, we will discuss public spirit and volunteering. As you continue to read, you will also get to know who should volunteer. Volunteering has challenges too, and it is good to know that and to be prepared to face those challenges as a good citizen.

Volunteer efforts, both individual and collective, play a remarkable role in addressing challenges facing societies all over the world. Those efforts continue to have a considerable impact, especially when it comes to addressing the needs of the downtrodden. Volunteering is an integral part of the social development policy of a given country. Of course, not everyone likes to volunteer. Volunteering is achieved by those who are public spirited. Winston Churchill once said that you make a living by what you get, but you create a life by what you provide.

Moving forward in this chapter, you need to answer some questions as a true citizen of this country concerning public spirit. Do you see South Sudan as your own country, of which you are proud and would do anything to protect? Do you care for its inhabitants, both living and non-living things? If you see garbage by the roadside or littering your town, do you see the need to remove it? Think about these questions as you continue to read this chapter to the end.

You need to take a look at your town's hygiene and sanitation and see if there is something you can do in your capacity to make it look good and healthy. When I talk about your capacity, I mean your ability to do the work, whether alone or by mobilizing others to help you. Showing unselfish interest in public welfare while disregarding your advantages and welfare over those of others is the actual demonstration of public-spiritedness. A public-spirited person always tries to help the community that they belong to.

Understanding Public Spirit

If you see suffering people on the street and you have remorse for their plight, then you are a public-spirited person. Indeed, the essence of public spirit is to be sympathetic to the citizens with more emphasis on the poor and to see all the inhabitants, both human and other living things, as important.

Many years ago, I used to see the church visiting the sick in the hospital while carrying soft drinks, food, and other edible things. Sometimes, they would also mobilize clothes and distribute them to the most vulnerable people in the community who could not afford to buy clothes. Such compassion is necessitated by the biblical call to care for the sick and the poor. If we can do this once in a while, we are fulfilling our public-spiritedness.

Promotion of public-spiritedness can also be achieved through the involvement of the local community in preventing revenge killing, cattle raids, and other crimes. Such activities should be done informally and with flexibility to realize better results. When the community and the government trust each other, both can achieve more. When you hear of civilians refusing to share information with the government, it means that trust is missing in that situation. As such, both the government and civilians have to build confidence and trust for the good of the country.

Who Should Volunteer?

There is no single citizen or group of people designated by any institution to perform voluntary work. Volunteering is entirely up to an individual's or group's spirit to do public good for the benefit of everyone. Such a spirit means that you have the ownership of your country at heart and a burning desire to see it progressing.

There is no particular person who owns this country. All of us own it together, and we all have a duty and responsibility to play our part in making it great. This can be achieved by empowering the people about their fundamental rights, safeguarding public properties, providing clean drinking water, improving sanitation, supporting the educational development, avoiding bribes, and maintaining the rule of law, among other things.

Success can be realized if we reject being guided by self-interest and prefer to work for the welfare of the public. History has proven that where there is a will among the citizens to work for the public good voluntarily, a country always grows at light speed. However, where there is no will, the government has a responsibility to encourage and remind the citizens to respond to this national call.

The government has to spare at least one day each month for citizens to undertake local community and neighborly activities. National and/or state-level campaigns encouraging the citizens to perform voluntary work should be created and spearheaded by state and local authorities.

The media and the church or mosque, through their wider coverage, should reach out to the community and mobilize them to perform voluntary duties. Promotion of the public good defines their existence as a medium of communication everywhere.

The government also has a responsibility to establish voluntary organizations or to influence the behavior of the citizens as part of its contribution to the welfare of the nation. In 1960, while John F. Kennedy was campaigning for the presidency in the United States of America, he was impressed by youngsters at the University of Michigan, who requested that he form the Peace Corps, where youth can work in different countries. Without wasting time, he accepted the idea and implemented it.

On September 22, 1961, the US Congress approved a budget of US$40 million for the establishment of the Peace Corps. It was a successful experiment, as it grew to operate in almost every part of the country, as well as internationally. Today there are Peace Corps in many parts of the world. The organization currently has a footprint in about 125 countries covering all the continents of the globe.

At the moment, the goal of the Peace Corps is no longer restricted to supporting the welfare of the American people but also provides technical assistance to other nations in order to bolster their social and economic development. In the same vein, the Peace Corps also aims to promote mutual understanding between Americans and the natives of the countries where the program serves.

In addition to the government, organizations have a responsibility to emerge and fill the gap that is left open. In South Sudan, some organizations such as youth bodies have already started to prove a point, although they are not sustainable enough, given the inconsistency of funds from the donors. Occasionally, they voluntary mobilize and collect the dirt littering the streets of Juba. That is a perfect start that only needs to be extended to other localities. Besides leisure time, companies, organizations, and governmental institutions can also create voluntary activities to promote public spirit at the workplace. This can engage those who use their leisure time for a rest, since public-spiritedness is not a force.

In our culture, women, including those serving in public offices, work longer hours than men in addition to performing household chores. Since women are already doing much more work then men at all levels, there is an opportunity for men to contribute more in this regard. It has to be noted that any strategy designed to foster public-spiritedness should be acceptable to all.

Recent research shows that one obvious and general rationale for using volunteers is that it is a cost-effective way to deliver services to the society. This does not mean that all volunteering work and service are for free. In some instances, there is a transaction cost to the volunteer, such as time commuting to and from the organization where one offers voluntary service. For some categories of volunteers, there are also volunteer living allowances and transportation costs, among others. There are different methods used to estimate the actual cost or economic value of a volunteer hour. Economically, the intention is to improve the quality of service while reducing costs. Economic evaluation of the net benefits of hospital volunteers best describes this strategy.

There is also a cost-saving effect of volunteering, as demonstrated by most studies in recent years. An economic evaluation of paid, volunteer, and mixed staffing options for public services is crucially important for a society to know why, how, and when to use volunteer labor resources. This interchangeability of paid staff and volunteers in nonprofit organizations gives an excellent organizational analysis for nonprofit management, including the value of volunteering for a nonprofit membership association.

The focus on the economic value risks overlooking the possibility that volunteers might provide unique advantages that would be harder to obtain with paid workers. Today, what is known about volunteering is that it has positive effects on communities and on the volunteers themselves. While a few have a low opinion of the practice, many believe that volunteering has important social values for society. Through volunteering, resources that are present within a society are deployed for the benefit of that society. While social capital is being redeemed, it is also being strengthened.

Volunteers are involved in the provision of social support at both meso and micro levels. At the meso level, such support involves organizations and networks that arrange for the provision of social support by individuals. This particular type of support is crucially important, since only a portion of all social support is provided spontaneously. On the other hand, support at the micro level consists of assistance that individual citizens provide to people in their surroundings. With this contrast, we have to agree that there is considerable variation in the range of support offered, as well as in the relationships underlying the support provided.

Whether services are provided by the unpaid volunteers or by the incentivized ones, beneficiaries are always the chief target cluster of the welfare work. To be a good citizen, it is of paramount importance to understand this and abide by the principles of volunteering.

Since the introduction of New Public Management in the 1980s, efficiency has been one of the main parameters used to evaluate social services. With the more recent development of evidence-based practice, the effectiveness of volunteering has come to the fore. Yet in contrast to these measures of the worth of volunteering to the communities and volunteers, very little thought is given to the price of volunteering to the beneficiaries of the services.

By volunteering, individuals learn civic skills, improve their social capital, and prevent social isolation. In addition to enhancing individual skills, volunteering contributes to the expansion of individual social capital. In the wake of individualization, people do not necessarily volunteer entirely to assist others but to support themselves as well. That is the growing sentiment everywhere.

By volunteering, individuals come into contact with more people, including those from other backgrounds than they would have encountered if they had not volunteered. This provides volunteers with larger social networks, as well as access to resources present within these expanded networks.

There are different perspectives on the value of volunteering. When volunteers learn basic social skills, it makes it easier for them to participate actively in societal activities. According to the Campaign to End Loneliness, it is believed that volunteering contributes to the prevention of social isolation, especially in old age. By volunteering, people become part of a social network.

For us to fulfill our vocation, no man should be excused from the full performance of his public duty, whether civil, political, or military. Remember, the Spartans of Ancient Greece were barbarous people, but they held and enforced one principle, which was essential to the existence of a republic: they believed that all men owed their first duty to the republic, from which nothing could excuse them. Good citizens know this secret, and that is why we should volunteer and make our country look great.

Challenges of Volunteering

The advantages of volunteering are much more significant than its disadvantages, but everything has both advantages and disadvantages. One of the dangers I would like to single out here in the use of volunteer campaigns for political purposes by individuals with such aspirations. This happened in Kenya after the deadly post-election violence of 2007.

In the immediate aftermath of Kenya's general elections in 2007, communities turned against one another in what observers would describe as ethnicization of politics. Some citizens felt that votes had been rigged. This discontentment sparked ethnic violence, which claimed thousands of lives. As a result, the youth who saw themselves as nationalists formed what they called "Youth Caravan."

This entity was a civil society organization (CSO) working to advocate for the national unity of all citizens divided by post-election violence. They would move from place to place to disseminate peace messages through rallies, sporting events, and concerts. Sometimes they organized cultural extravaganzas where communities would showcase their cultures.

A few months before the 2010 elections, some politicians who were contesting for various positions in the government approached the leadership of this civil society organization, wanting it to support them in their campaigns through such activities as drama and musical performance. The leadership of the organization turned down their requests and explained to the politicians that they were not a political entity but a voluntary organization working to promote national unity.

As we speak, the Youth Caravan is still alive and considered as an important CSO in Kenya because it resisted the temptation of campaigning for politicians. This could have tarnished their good reputation as a non-partisan entity if they had allowed themselves to be lured by the politicians into campaigning for them at the expense of their mission of setting the country on the right course after the bloody ethnic violence.

Civil society organizations are always respected for their impartiality in political settings and usually expected to spearhead voluntary service campaigns. Through the mobilization of international as well as local volunteers, CSOs can engage the community and help them in the delivery of constructive messages about peace, reconciliation, and civic partici-pation at all levels of the government. If local volunteers are equipped and empowered, they can serve as interlocutors between different warring parties in post-conflict environments, provided that they abide by a "do no harm" approach streamlined into the United Nations (UN) system's entire programs, operations, and interventions the world over.

In situations where the UN mission is about to phase out of the country, local entities, especially civil societies, are always capacitated and prepared to bridge the gap caused by the UN mission's departure. In spite of such an important interlocutory role, they are still seen by the parties to the conflict as partisans, simply because they are run by nationals.

In general terms, history has proven that politicization of voluntary service always kills the spirit of volunteerism itself. Because of this, we should let the public virtue and the intelligence of the people be constantly inculcated by the press, the school, and the church until the whole nation is fully educated about the maximum and solemn duty of regenerating the social institutions of humankind. When that is done, then we will be able to pause, relax, and say the mission is finally accomplished.

SIX

EXERCISE OF VOTING RIGHTS

"Elections belong to the people. It's their decision.
If they decide to turn their back on the fire and burn their behinds,
then they will have to sit on their blisters."
Abraham Lincoln

IN THE PREVIOUS CHAPTER, we discussed public spirit and volunteering. By the time you finished that chapter, I believe you have learned about the importance of volunteering, who should volunteer, and the challenges facing volunteering. In this chapter, we are going to discuss one of the essential topics related to good citizenship, and that is the exercise of voting rights, which has been a popular demand of people all over the world for so many years. As you continue to read, you will learn about the benefits of voting and get to know what electorates expect from their representatives as they elect them into office.

Before we do that, let's first understand the origin and definition of the word "election." The words "elect" and "election" have their origins in two Latin words: e, which means "out of," and lectus, which means "chosen." Therefore, the successful candidates in any general election are literally "chosen out of" the people who stand for various seats during the election. An election is understood as a formal group decision-making process by which a population chooses an individual to hold a public office.

Back in history, the concept of election had its origin in ancient Athens and the Holy Roman Empire. In ancient Athens, the election was considered an oligarchic institution, and most political offices were filled using sortation, also known as allotment, by which office-holders were chosen by lot. In the Holy Roman Empire, it was used in the selection of popes and emperors.

Since the seventeenth century, it has been used as a mechanism by which modern representative democracy operates, as it is used to fill offices in different branches of government at both national and local levels. The election process is also used in the private sector, particularly in business organizations, as well as in voluntary associations. In modern representative democracies, the universal use of elections as a tool for selecting representatives contrasts with the practice in ancient Athens.

The vote is considered a sacred trust in the hands of the citizens that should always be used judiciously. While the basic idea of voting is fairly universal, the method by which those votes are used to determine a winner can vary depending on context and setting. In many decision-making processes, it is necessary to gather the group consensus to determine a course of action. Among a group of friends, you may decide upon a movie by voting for all the movies you're willing to watch, with the winner being the one with the greatest approval. A company may jettison unpopular schemes, then re-vote on the remaining options. A country may look for a candidate with the leading number of votes. In deciding upon a winner, there is always one main goal, which is to reflect the preferences of the people in the fairest way possible.

Suitable representatives should be sent to the parliament to champion the citizens' agenda. Voting is the only way to ensure representatives whose wisdom may best discern the true interest of our country, and whose patriotism and love of justice may serve as a flagship in moving the country forward. If we use it wisely, our vote could bind us together even more than our history of striving for freedom and liberty. Our bond of exercising our free will for a better life can be a guarantee for our rights as stipulated in our constitution. Whether you agree with me or not, our vote is the strongest tool we have to protect and maintain our freedom to live as we choose.

Throughout history, people have had to fight hard for their right to vote, and some have even died for it, though it has become a right we surely take for granted today. In Australia, for instance, women weren't allowed to vote in the elections until 1923. For them to be able to cast their votes, a group of powerful women known as suffragettes protested hard for the democratic right that women enjoy today. However, that was not the end of the story, but only the beginning, as Aboriginal Australians still couldn't enjoy that right to vote. These indigenous people struggled for ages until 1962, when they finally achieved voting rights.

In the United States, so many marginalized groups throughout history have battled for the right to vote through protests and civil rights movements. Women weren't allowed to vote until 1920, and they still wouldn't be able to today if it weren't for the thousands of people who bravely took part in the women's suffrage movement. You might have heard of Martin Luther King, Jr., as well, who championed civil rights for black Americans, including the right to vote.

In the old Sudan, casting votes was complicated for political and security reasons. Our fathers and grandfathers never enjoyed the right to vote. Maybe your great-grandmother was a suffragette, or your great-uncle was an activist. You also have to understand that over 2.5 million people died in the struggle for self-determination to achieve freedom and democracy. Think about how they would feel if you couldn't go to a polling booth. Without the vote of a free man, we are but slaves without the power to make decisions.

Many of us sometimes give unreasonable excuses to avoid the ballot, even something as simple as a change in the weather on the voting day. As you wake up in the morning to go for a vote, you may be slapped in the face with frigid weather. The morning may look like those days where you have to force yourself to go to class over the temptation of hibernating in your bedroom and waiting for the sunrise to clear the dew.

In a situation where you find yourself feeling lazy, you may tell yourself that there is always a "next time" for you to cast your vote. However, being ignorant in an election season is dangerous, as there is no guarantee that you will reach the "next time." It may turn out that the opponent narrowly beats your favorite candidate because you did not want to walk in the dew to vote. The candidate that succeeded in the election may then decide to amend the constitution and remove term limits, thereby taking away your chance to vote against that candidate the "next time." Since it would be too late for you to cast your vote, the end result would be a feeling of guilt for your indecision.

Whereas you are so lucky to be able to cast your vote, there are countries that, even today, make it difficult for citizens to vote. While they are probably amazing countries in a lot of ways, the people who live there don't have the same voting rights you have, as they live under dictatorial rule. Since you are free and have the choice to cast your vote, the only thing you should do is to choose wisely for your candidate.

One of the most annoying things is the failure of the energetic youth and ignorant older adults to cast their votes. If these people actually register and tell politicians what they think, it will almost certainly change the outcome of every election. Such an outcome could mean surviving economic crises, finding affordable housing, or being able to find a decent job.

Young people are the inventors, the digital content creators, the athletes, musicians, artists, and students that represent our generation, as they are energetic and capable of changing the world. In today's world, young people are the ones pushing society forward. Moreover, whether they like it or not, they are the ones who will have to live with the results of every election. Therefore, they need to seize the opportunity and exercise their power to vote.

You might have heard of the term "aging population." In developed countries, people are having fewer kids and living longer. In this situation, the population is made up of more older people than younger people. This is significant because while older people generally want comfort and stability, the younger generations push for change. To be honest with you, the only way things will change politically is when young people become politically engaged. This begins with everyone who turns eighteen registering to vote in an election. However, such a quest for change should not be done violently to disrupt the functionality of the state institutions.

We sometimes fear that, to quote US President James Madison, "men of factious tempers, of local prejudices, or of sinister designs, may, by intrigue, by corruption, or by other means, first obtain the suffrages, and then betray the interests, of the people." This should not kill our spirit to go to the polls, because change does not come overnight. The only thing that should kill your spirit is your failure to vote and your ignorance and lack of self-awareness. You have to understand that your silence is the approval for bad leaders to rule you. To guard against unworthy candidates and the vicious arts of politics, we have to choose the most attractive merit and established characters, as the improper use of the vote may result in a bad government.

What Electorates Expect from Their Representatives

Members of Parliament have a responsibility to three main groups: their constituents, Parliament, and their political party. Each MP is elected to the national Parliament or state legislative assembly by his or her constituents. In Parliament, MPs' duties include participating in debates and voting on legislation and other matters. Some may be selected to head a specialized committee to examine new laws or the work of government departments. Others are absorbed into the executive to serve as ministers in the government.

MPs also have a role in helping their constituents by advising them on problems, particularly those that arise from the work of government departments. They also represent the concerns of their constituents in the Parliament by acting as a figurehead for their localities. Members of Parliament usually support their political parties by voting with their leadership in the Parliament. Moreover, they act as representatives for the party in their respective constituencies.

In all countries where representatives are elected to offices by citizens, electorates have a lot of expectations for their leaders. Those expectations always make the representatives act in response to various pressures, since they are obligated to fulfill their electorates' demands in the hope of being re-elected. In democracies, good representatives are seen as delegates addressing constituent concerns and the competing demands of their people, or as those who advocate, enact, and pass bills that change the lives of all citizens. Concisely, democratic representation is characterized by regular free and fair elections, with citizens evaluating good and/or bad representation.

Pessimists argue that re-election does not mean that the representative has been a good representative, as the electorates sometimes end up sending to Parliament people who cannot advocate for their cause or render the necessary services. However, optimists still maintain the belief that doing what the electorates think is best for them as a representative can be a sure ticket to re-election.

If you contested and you lose the election, and you think that you are capable, maintain that positive spirit. There are many examples the world over where defeated parliamentarians have still been regarded as outstanding representatives, and vice versa, despite losing terribly. US President Abraham Lincoln is a historic example of perseverance, as he experienced numerous setbacks and defeats, both personal and political, before winning the presidency of the United States of America. Today, he is remembered as one of the greatest presidents in the history of the United States. Persist and people will still come back for you tomorrow if you choose to be wholesome.

In my life, I have seen governors and Members of Parliament who terribly lost the elections and constitutional post holders who were relieved of their posts, yet they made a political comeback. Some of them even made it back more than two times. In politics, everyone is useful at his or her own pace. It is the same with the sun and the moon, which shine during their own times. During the daytime, we think that there is nothing darker to overshadow the daytime light. However, when night comes, the moon will appear from nowhere and light the darker night. This universal rule is reflected in the human character too. You can be a good leader during peacetime, but in times of crisis, your approach may not be suitable for stabilizing the conflict situation.

During a crisis or in a conflict situation, leaders are required to make hard decisions to quell the situation. Softness is not bad, as it is one of the important traits required of a good leader during peacetime. However, this has to be balanced during a crisis, as there are situations where bold decisions are required.

One of my good friends was relieved from the county commissionership position and was later elevated to a ministerial position at the state level. This commissioner is not only a great Christian but also a pastor in his denomination. He is highly educated and served in various senior positions in the past, including being a state prison police director and a chaplain, among others.

While interacting with another one of my friends, a senior government official, to understand the reason for the commissioner's removal from the county commissionership position, he told me the commissioner was relieved because some elements from his community went to the governor and lobbied for his removal because they felt that he was not addressing their individual needs. I took a particular interest in listening to the charges leveled against him. However, most of these charges had nothing to do with his public responsibility as head of the county.

One of the claims was connected to his refusal of the unnecessary killing of cows for casual dinners. They claim that he does not allow for the killing of cows in his house, nor does he allow purposeless gathering in his house. Whenever the community tells him a cow should be slaughtered, he would ask them, "What has the cow done wrong for us to shed its blood?" Others mentioned that he does not give cash for the purchase of cigarettes and that whenever you ask him for a cigarette, he would tell you, "Smoking is a sin before God." Some said he doesn't provide alcohol when you pay him a visit. They further claimed that he hardly avails himself to the community on Saturdays because, being part of the Seventh-day Adventist Church, he devotes that day to prayers.

To those who know the commissioner better, he is a good citizen who does not work only for the welfare of his county but also for that of his state and the whole nation. He is not just a leader for a few individuals who only seek some money for tobacco or alcohol for their individual interests or needs; his interest is beyond that. He works to transform the county as a whole.

A few days after his appointment as a county commissioner, he mobilized the community to carry out general cleaning in the town, especially in the county's biggest market. He made cleaning a routine voluntary activity in the county, with volunteers gathering to clean the town every weekend. He is a good citizen based on the values you are reading about in this book.

In chapter five, you read about volunteering. One of the volunteer's roles is the cleaning of the environment, which is precisely what the commissioner had been doing. He managed to mobilize the community to make their surrounding environment clean voluntarily, and this qualifies him to be a good citizen.

Benefits of Voting

Voting is believed to have a host of positive benefits for the individual voter who turns out to the polls to cast their votes. These benefits range from social connection and active citizenship to personal action.

If we compare voters with non-voters, it is likely that voters have more contact with their elected officials than non-voters. Through such connections, they become well informed about local and national affairs, as they have an interest in knowing how their country is being managed.

Personal Action

In our daily lives, action is more important than words. If you are a person of action, you are always happy even when your activity does not bear fruit. Taking action is a motivating factor in itself. For this reason, voters have the satisfaction of knowing that they have expressed their opinions whenever they cast their votes. Voting is a form of personal empowerment that gives you the opportunity to voice your opinion on issues that matter to you, your family, your community, and your country.

Psychologist Marc Zimmerman, a professor at the University of Michigan's School of Health in the United States, argues that those who cast their votes in an election are happier with the outcome because they feel they are in control of their lives even if the winner of an election was not their preferred choice. This is because voting has other benefits such as social connections, proof of active citizenship, and personal agency.

There are countries that went through tough times as sections of the population were denied voting rights. In the United States, for example, the Voting Rights Act that allowed African-Americans to exercise their voting rights was only signed into law in 1965 by President Lyndon B. Johnson. It was a milestone achievement in the fight for equal civil rights among the black community, as it aimed to overcome legal barriers at the state and local levels that prevented African-Americans from exercising their right to vote as bonded under the Fifteenth Amendment to the U.S. Constitution. The Civil Rights Act of 1964 hastened the end of the legal segregation of black people, popularly known as "Jim Crow," as it secured African-Americans equal access to restaurants, transportation, and other public facilities. The end of Jim Crow also enabled blacks, women, and other minorities to break down barriers in the workplace.

When South Sudanese voted for the first time during the referendum for self-determination that seceded the region from the Sudan in fulfillment of the 2005 Comprehensive Peace Agreement, people from all walks of life were jubilant and celebrated even before the results were released. The excitement was birthed by the sense of freedom, as many had never had a chance to exercise their full voting rights under the successive Sudanese regimes. This is an affirmation that a person's action to vote is a pride to the voter everywhere in the world.

Social Connections

Social connection is an essential thing for all human beings. We are inherently social creatures, and for that reason, when we are not connected, we feel bored, frustrated, and even depressed. Even before recorded history, there is evidence of humans moving and working in social groups, often suffering severe consequences if separated from their tribe.

Studies suggest that voters tend to have stronger social connections that lead to a more exceptional quality of life and longevity during and after the election process. This is more likely to be true in countries with a strong democratic system where it's difficult to rig the elections. In such a situation, politicians find it dangerous to detach themselves from their constituents, since doing so would mean losing in the next election. Such representatives also work very hard to provide social services to their communities. Provision of services could mean honest fulfilment of the electoral campaign promises, or it could be a sign of an early campaign for a future election.

Registered voters are also said to be more connected to their neighbors and family members as compared to non-voters. This is because they are likely to discuss political, social, and developmental issues with family, representatives, and the broader community members who share specific ideas with them.

Social grouping is more crucial than ever, as it provides us with a vital part of our identity, and more than that, it teaches us to feel connected, particularly in this increasingly isolated world. The benefits of social connectedness improve our quality of life and should not be overlooked. Indeed, if you have ever moved away from your familiar social environment and settled elsewhere, you must have a good idea of how much your everyday life and wellbeing depend on social connections.

One study found that social connection has a greater effect on health than such factors as obesity, smoking, and high blood pressure. Social connection doesn't just refer to being around people physically, but also to whether someone feels understood and connected to others. The UCLA Loneliness Scale can be used to determine a person's subjective level of loneliness.

Social connection has also been confirmed to improve mental health. For instance, the mental health benefits of friendship include improvements in confidence, happiness, and feelings of belonging, as well as reductions in stress levels. One study in Buffalo, New York, found a link between a lack of social support and mental health disorders such as anxiety and depression.

Social connections can also improve physical health and longevity. A 2010 review of more than 100 studies on the subject concluded that stronger social relationships were associated with a 50 percent increased likelihood of survival, independent of such factors as age, sex, initial health status, and cause of death.

Another vital benefit of connection is related to decreasing the risk of suicide. Connectedness is one of many factors that can increase or decrease a person's risk of suicide. People who are hopeless in life opt to take out the life in them. It is believed that relationships can play a crucial role in protecting a person against suicidal thoughts and behaviors if they are observed and taken care of prior to their action.

Active Citizenship

In any country, there are always two types of citizens: active citizens and passive citizens. Passive citizens are those who are not very opinionated about the affairs of their country, especially how it is run or managed. They don't bother themselves with the latest issues of their country, including voting in an election. This category of citizens feels that voting is a waste of time, as it makes no difference in their lives. They think that even if they vote, their candidate may not win or be allowed to ascend to power by the prevailing political circumstances surrounding the electoral process. Others who have no interest in politics at all see it as unimportant and unwise to waste their valuable time on something with no value to them.

On the other hand, active citizens are the ones who take part in any development or activity that requires civic participation in their country. Registered voters fall in this category, as they are proactive and mindful about all the happenings within their community or the country as a whole. In most cases, they engage in more civic and political activities than those who are not registered, whom we refer to as passive citizens.

Active citizens, in most cases, take the initiative to talk to their elected representatives and advocate for developmental projects in their communities after the election. Electorates are required to be engaged citizens who connect with their representatives and neighbors, and who participate in social and civic activities for the betterment of their country.

In some situations, especially in countries where migrants are numerous, citizens find themselves being excluded in political processes as well as in day-to-day life. A 2014 research study on "active citizenship, participation, and belonging" carried out by the Center for Multicultural Youth in Victoria, Australia, found that young people from migrant and refugee backgrounds often feel excluded not only from mainstream political processes but also from day-to-day levels of participation. This research argues that the complex range of barriers young people from migrant and refugee backgrounds often encounter can result in their being unable to shape their own lives as they had hoped, resulting in feelings of frustration, disempowerment, and ostracism.

It has been observed in some countries where voting is compulsory that registered voters with little interest in voting show up to the polling stations and tick the voting slip carelessly without caring about who they have voted for. People in this group vote only to avoid being fined by the government for not voting. They constitute what I would best call "less active citizens." To them, the electoral process is so confusing that they do not know who to vote for, who is responsible for what, and the different tiers of government in which candidates are contesting for political office. For active citizenship to be realized, it is crucially important to involve everyone in the running of the country's affairs with more emphasis on elections. Citizens need to go through civic education so that they know what it means to be a voter.

SEVEN

TOLERANCE

"Tolerance is the positive and cordial effort to understand another's beliefs,
practices, and habits without necessarily sharing or accepting them."
Joshua Liebman

IN CHAPTER SIX, WE DISCUSSED the exercise of voting rights, its benefits, and the expectations of electorates for their representatives. In this chapter, we will talk about the importance of tolerance and its effects on citizens.

Toleration is defined as a fair, objective, and permissive attitude toward those whose opinions, beliefs, practices, or racial or ethnic origins, among other factors, differ from one's own. It is the acceptance of an action, object, or person whom one dislikes or disagrees with. British mathematician Jacob Bronowski described tolerance as "the essential safeguard, the essential degree of coarseness, which makes it possible to work with abstract entities in the real world." We are living in a world where conflict is a salient feature of human society. Everywhere you go, you will find that men fight among themselves even with their bare fists if they do not possess arms or other tools of violence. Such conflicts that always manifest in disagreement, anger, quarrel, hatred, destruction, killing, or war are believably caused by greed, covetousness, self-centeredness, discontent, envy, arrogance, rudeness, or impunity, among other acts.

Twentieth-century English philosopher Bertrand Russell, once argued that the world should be turned into a "scientific society," where wars are abolished, population growth is limited, and prosperity is shared. He went further to suggest the establishment of a "single supreme world government" capable of enforcing peace. He considered cooperation as the only thing that could redeem humankind. If these criteria were met, according to him, individuals could grow freely, as hate, envy, and greed would vanish because there would be nothing to nourish them.

Mahatma Gandhi once said, "The whole world is like the human body with its various members. Pain in one member is felt in the whole body." He saw violence as a bad way to demand one's rights or advance the group's interest. For that matter, he argued that it is only by gentle means that one could shake the world. That is why he believed firmly in non-violence. Tolerance is the only thing that could enable people belonging to different backgrounds to live together as one people.

Intolerance is not only evil, but it is also capable of producing a breakdown of human relations in societies where it is the story of the day. In practical life, different types of tolerance occur most often in our daily life as we interact with one another. In this chapter, I will focus on two types of tolerance: unilateral and bilateral. Let's start by understanding the prefixes. Uni means one, and bi means two. If one group allows another to celebrate its culture and exercise its religious practices, but not the reverse, that would be an example of unilateral tolerance. For instance, a particular Christian country might allow mosques to be built, but Christians may not have the same privilege in an Islamic country. The second type is bilateral tolerance. For instance, in a marriage, if the husband and wife both permit relationships outside of their marriage, that would be an example of bilateral tolerance. We sometimes expect others to tolerate our views of a particular matter, like politics and life choices, yet when someone is living out their own life choices or political views, we impose and even obstruct their right and ability to make those choices.

In another sense, tolerance is seen as being patient, understanding, and accepting of anything different. We say there is tolerance when an individual accepts the existence of different opinions than their own and doesn't take adverse steps to eliminate them or aggressively show their resentment against them. A living example of this type of tolerance is when Muslims, Christians, and atheists view themselves as friends rather than enemies. We cannot all be of the same faith, and this is a fact that we cannot change. As the theologian Reinhold Niebuhr famously said, we need to have the serenity to accept the things that we cannot change, the courage to change the things we can, and the wisdom to know the difference.

Being tolerant of each other and caring for one another is what makes us true humans. By teaching tolerance, we allow individuality and diversity while promoting peace and harmony in our society. Our success in the struggle against intolerance depends on the effort we make in educating ourselves and our youngsters about the importance of peaceful coexistence and social cohesion among our communities.

In today's world, our understanding of tolerance has been poisoned by political sycophancy and thirst for material needs. When we compare traditional and modern forms of tolerance, we will find that traditional tolerance is far more important. Traditional tolerance values respect and accepts the individual without necessarily approving of or participating in his or her beliefs or behaviors. Traditional tolerance differentiates between what an individual thinks or does and the person himself.

Sometimes we tend to confuse secularism with religious tolerance. Secularism is the principle of the separation of government institutions and individuals mandated to represent the state from religious institutions and spiritual dignitaries, whereas religious tolerance is about allowing others to hold dogmas that are divergent to one's own beliefs. It does not require that opposing beliefs be facilitated, supported, or not contradicted, but it does require that competing beliefs be allowed to exist. Religious tolerance additionally means permitting others to think, follow, or practice their religions and philosophies without interference. In a country with a state religion, toleration means that the government allows other religions to be practiced there. Others permit public faith, yet apply non-secular or religious discrimination in different ways.

The main point of difference between these two is that religious tolerance is more of a negative concept, where you tolerate the person with different religious beliefs than your own, which sometimes goes against the spirit of our Constitution. On the other hand, secularism is more of a positive concept, which means more than the tolerance of other religions and includes respect for their religious beliefs too. This principle is based on fraternity and is in line with our Constitution.

In the workplace, tolerance helps employees build bridges and capitalize on the differences present, such as those related to diverse cultural backgrounds. Most organizations lay out a zero-tolerance policy to help guide workers on issues related to unacceptable behaviors in the workplace. Tolerance is neither indulgence nor indifference; it is respect or appreciation for our rich and diverse cultures, our forms of countenance, and our ways of being human.

Children are the future of this country, and we have to inculcate tolerance in them such that they feel special, safe, and loved. We should not spare words of praise or affection if we want them to become good citizens when they grow up. In this way, we should teach them about new places, people, and cultures. We should also expose them to different perspectives through books, music, food, and cultural events. Since humans always feel good when they are praised, we should use positive comments to shape and reinforce their behaviors too.

Importance of Tolerance

One of the best examples of the importance of tolerance is Nelson Mandela. After he became the President of South Africa, he once asked members of his close protection to stroll with him in the city and have lunch at one of the restaurants. They entered and sat in one of the downtown restaurants, where they asked for some food.

After a short moment, the waiter brought them their orders. He noticed that someone was sitting in front of his table, also waiting for food. He then told one of his bodyguards to go and ask the man who was sitting alone at the other corner of the restaurant hall to join them with his food so that they could eat together at the same table. The soldier went and asked the man, who complied with the request. The man came with his food and sat by Mandela's side as he began to eat. This man's hands were constantly trembling, from the moment he joined the table until everyone finished eating. When he finished his food, he sought permission and he was allowed to go.

After he had left, the soldier said to President Mandela that the man must be sick because his hands trembled as he ate. "No, not at all," said Mandela. "This man was one of the guards in the prison where I was jailed for several years. Often, after the torture I was subjected to, I used to scream and ask for a little water. This exact man used to come every time and urinate on my head instead of giving me the water I asked for. Therefore, I found him frightened and trembling, thinking that I would now retaliate, at least in the same manner, either by torturing him or by imprisoning him, as I am now the President of the State of South Africa. However, this is not my character nor part of my ethics."

Mandela had this in mind. He understood that the mentality of retaliation destroys states, while the mentality of tolerance builds nations. He also noted that tolerance for one another's views creates a peaceful condition, which gives space for the best in all people to find expression and flourish. Forgiveness and tolerance are his principles, which he also acknowledged immediately after his release from the prison when he said, "As I walked out the door toward the gate that would lead to my freedom, I knew if I didn't leave my bitterness and hatred behind, I would still be in prison." If Mandela were vengeful, this prison warden would have faced the consequences of his previous action. However, as a good citizen, Mandela realized that forgiveness and tolerance are the essence of nation-building and there is no point in retaliating.

Important parts of developing a more tolerant outlook are learning to appreciate and value our differences, accepting uncertainties, learning about other people and their cultures, analyzing our intolerant feelings, fostering our self-esteem, and thinking challenging thoughts. We are living in a diverse country, a country inhabited by sixty-four tribes with different languages and cultures. Some have different beliefs and varied civilizations. How can we live together if we don't embrace each other? Is it possible to disband some tribes and pick one? Do we have to choose only one language, culture, religion, and civilization and disband the rest? Certainly, the answer is no. Well, now you have agreed with me that it is impossible, what can we do? Can we embrace one another the way we are now? I think so.

Diversity is essential, and countries that embrace it could tell you its benefits. Let me pick culture as an example of one of the differences we have, and share with you how beneficial it is. In the Bible, Jesus told his disciples, "I am using earthly parables because if I give a parable about heaven, none of you will understand it because no one has seen heaven among you." Having said this, I don't want to take you too far beyond our borders, so I will limit my example to Kenya's Maasai tribe.

Maasai in Kenya has a vibrant culture that attracts tourists to the country from all over the world. Their dance to the sky, which is almost similar to that of Atuot in South Sudan, has for decades boosted Kenya's economy as tourists leave their countries just to have a live look at this amazing modernized traditional dance rather than watching it on the BBC's or Al Jazeera's documentaries. When these tourists arrive in Kenya, they usually stay in hotels, eat local foods, and travel in cars not necessarily owned by Maasai but by other Kenyans. This means Maasai dance is beneficial to all Kenyans and not only to the Maasai. Many people do not understand this hidden truth because they fail to connect the dots. Kenyan citizens who understand the importance of Maasai culture cannot do harm to members of the Maasai tribe.

As South Sudanese, we need to appreciate our God-given differences because they are economically and socially beneficial to us in many ways. A diverse country is like a man with many types of weapons who hardly ever loses a battle because he is fortified. We should show tolerance towards one another. Our tribes, religions, race, and political divisions should not be allowed to fragment our social fabric. The religious belief that says, "Do unto others what you wish to be done to you," should be the motto of every citizen.

Effects of Intolerance

For almost a century, our communities have gone through turbulent times. Communities that neighbor each other have gone through the fiercest tribal fighting, cattle raids and counter cattle raids, revenge killing, child abduction, land-related conflict, and many more. Among the recurring conflicts is the cattle raid and counter cattle raid between Nuer and Dinka. According to legend, the cattle raid problem between Nuer and Dinka started a long time ago due to dishonesty between the two brothers.

The Dinka was an elder son, while the Nuer was the younger son. Their father was a responsible man in the village. One day in his old age, he called his two sons so that he could distribute his wealth to them. When his sons arrived, he began to tell them everything about life, including how they should live once he leaves their midst. Finally, he told them about his wealth. It has to be noted that all he had was one female cow and its calf, which was also a female. That was a lot during that time, as many people did not even have chickens, let alone goats. After they sat down on a papyrus mat while preparing to listen to the interesting part of the story related to wealth distribution, they began to be attentive. The room was quiet to such an extent that even the air respected their dire need for silence.

He cleared his throat in what seemed to be an attempt to make his voice heard as he read the decree of wealth distribution. In respect of seniority, he first started with Dinka. I do not know whether that is what they called themselves when they were brothers, or if they adopted those names decades later. "Dinka," he called, "I give you that cow; take it, and it is your share of my wealth." Dinka was reluctant, but he could not visibly express his discontentment to his aged father for giving him an old cow. With due respect, Dinka reluctantly said, "Yes, Dad, thank you, I will take it."

The older man turned to his younger son, Nuer, and said to him, "My son Nuer." "Yes, Dad," Nuer responded. "Take that female calf. It is your share of my wealth which I give to you." "Thank you, father," Nuer responded.

After the distribution of wealth, he told them to go. The two children parted ways; Dinka left with his cow to a certain village and built his home there, and Nuer went to a different village to start building his home.

Dinka was not contented with his cow. He felt that their father was not fair for giving the calf to his younger son while giving him an older cow. "Something must be wrong with my father," he said. "He must not love me. I will show them."

Months later, he made up his mind. He traveled to the village where his brother lived. Upon reaching the village, he refused to go home but scanned where the cows were grazing. To his luck, he saw the calf that was given to his brother by their old father. He hastily drove it away to his village.

In the evening, when the cows returned home, the calf was not there. Nuer wondered what had happened to his calf. He carried out a thorough search in the whole village, moving from home to home, kraal to kraal, and he could not locate its whereabouts.

The following morning, he went to the neighboring villages, but to no avail. He extended his search to the distant bushes and plains, and there was no calf. After he got tired, he came back home. He thought of what could have happened to his calf. An ocean of thoughts flooded his mind. First, he thought of wild animals who might have devoured his calf. However, he immediately canceled this thought, as he convinced himself that he would have found a trail of blood in the bush during his exhaustive search.

Finally, he made up his mind. He decided to go and visit his brother Dinka, whom he seriously suspected of stealing his calf. He recalled the time when his brother was reluctant to accept his share of the old cow when his father gave it to him during the wealth distribution. He set off for a journey and arrived the following morning at his brother's home. While approaching the home, he saw his bouncy calf. Without a word, he untied it.

While Nuer was doing that, his brother held the rope, thus igniting the fight between the two brothers. Although he managed to take his calf in the end, it is said that Dinka followed him and brought back the calf. That was the beginning of the cattle raid and counter cattle raid between Nuer and Dinka.

Today, Nuer and Dinka continue to carry out cattle raid and counter cattle raid on the pretext of recovering their once-stolen cattle. It is not clear when the two tribes are going to cease from this practice. If I were asked to give an opinion on how this persistent conflict should be resolved, I would recommend that the two brothers sit down and decide afresh on who should take the cow and who should go with the calf to end this epic.

In addition to the historical cattle raid and counter cattle raid between the two aforementioned tribes, the cycle of child abduction entangling Murle, Lou Nuer, and Dinka Bor is another worrisome scenario. For several decades, intercommunal conflicts triggered by child abduction have claimed so many lives. Different levels of government, various community peace structures, and humanitarian actors, both local and international, have been trying to curtail this precarious practice for several years, but all efforts always go in vain.

The land Saga between the Chollo and Dinka Abilang is another issue that requires an amicable solution. Additionally, in Raja, the conflict between the pastoralists and farmers requires national attention, as the issue is likely to threaten the social fabric of these communities. As citizens, we cannot afford to be against each other while we expect the country to be at peace. Unless we embrace one another, this country cannot be at peace with itself.

How to Tolerate Unacceptable Behavior

Tolerance is good in itself as it builds group cohesion. However, there are situations when one should break the silence. Let's take the example of sexual harassment in the workplace. A victim should not keep quiet because it will set a bad precedent in the company. You and I know that much has been written in recent years about why women, for instance, are reluctant to speak up after sexual harassment they have experienced, and why this type of unacceptable behavior is sometimes tolerated. They are afraid to come forward and stand up for themselves in such situations because they know if they do, they will be punished, ridiculed, shamed, and scorned by the surrounding society. Others fear that they will lose their livelihoods and be black-listed or fired from their workplaces. Sadly enough, this is even more the case when the abuser still holds a senior position in an institution. As a result, many people today, particularly women, keep themselves small and powerless.

There are other events or processes which are a part of everyone's life, such as the seemingly straightforward process of interviewing for a job, dealing with a noxious boss, or handling a friend who behaves offensively. Even in these everyday experiences, we can begin to see there are frequent, overarching reasons why individuals tolerate behaviors that keep them feeling insecure, petrified, and unworthy.

In this case, let's take interviewing as an example. In daily life, people will often wait for weeks or even months for feedback from the hiring manager or organization just because they feel afraid that asking for a response would look too pushy. Sometimes they will be tossed around like a pawn in the process, or be lied to or misled terribly, without ever speaking up and saying a thing about it to the offender.

In case you are undergoing this situation, don't allow external events to shrink your confidence, make you question your talents and experience, or at worst, bring you to your knees with self-doubt and feelings of worthlessness. A good citizen does not lose his self-worth when undergoing an intolerable situation. When dealing with chronically unacceptable behaviors, you need to put these four things in mind: knowing what is acceptable and what is not, demanding your right nonviolently, being engaged, and knowing your self-worth.

Know What is Acceptable and What is Not

In childhood, many people were taught terrible lessons that harmed them concerning what is acceptable and what is not. For instance, if you had emotionally manipulative or narcissistic parents or were abused in any way, you most likely were not able to develop sufficient and appropriate boundaries that allow you to say "no" to behavior that is violating, manipulative, and suppressing your values. As such, some people have chosen to work incredibly hard to be loved and accepted and never received the unconditional, nurturing love and acceptance they deserved. They had to compromise who they are — their values, beliefs, and integrity — to get what they needed. This is what makes them more susceptible as adults to tolerating behaviors that should not be allowed.

But even for those who were not mistreated or neglected in childhood, were they taught that it was okay to stand up for themselves and speak up to authority figures and others when something felt wrong? Were they able to trust their instincts and act on them? Did they get to know themselves deeply, to learn how to discern what feels wrong? In the absence of these, one needs to work very hard to see the difference between what she or he should accept and what she or he should not. Such a process of knowing oneself intimately, and honoring what one believes and feels is right, requires bravery and courage.

Demand Your Right Nonviolently

Many people, including those I know, do understand that the behavior they're experiencing is wrong and shouldn't be tolerated, but they just can't muster the strength to say or do anything about it. This is because they have allowed the fear of their actions to overcome them. This has to change.

If you feel you cannot address a negative or unacceptable behavior by yourself, you'd better reach out and get some outside help. You don't have to be violent while responding to the situation affecting you. Calculate your moves and act emotionlessly without the temptation to cause violence.

You can even ask a mentor who is safe and whom you respect and trust for support in such a situation. If not, find an influential lawyer who is an expert in what you are dealing with. Do not stop there; go ahead and consult a therapist to intervene too. Don't attempt to stay silent. By all means, speak up, get out of the vacuum that has become your life, and get some powerful outside help to shift your current situation for the better.

Some people were active in the past and spoke up for themselves, but have been punished for doing so, and don't want that behavior repeated. Today, thousands of women in our world, for instance, are retaliated against for being forceful, assertive, and brave. Gender bias is real and alive, and the perceived value and competency of women has been shown to fall dramatically when they are viewed as forceful or intense.

In March 2020, an analysis on gender social norms carried out by the United Nations Development Programme (UNDP), including data from 75 countries representing 80 percent of the world's population, revealed a shocking scale of global women's rights backlash. The research showed that 90 percent of people are biased against women, as the individuals interviewed held at least one bias against women in relation to politics, economics, education, violence, or reproductive rights. Almost half of people interviewed were so blind on gender parity that they feel men are superior political leaders than women. Additionally, more than 40 percent believe that men make better business executives than women.

As we have seen in many studies, success and likability are positively correlated for men while they are negatively correlated for women; this unconscious bias has a crushing impact on the lives of those who are discriminated against whenever nothing is done to correct it.

These stereotypes are not true, and women should not think that they are second-class humans. They are great leaders, and some of them are even more capable then men. Good men always respect and recognize the role women are playing in the society. They also support women when they are fighting for their rights.

Women should not give up the fight against gender inequality. If you have been punished in the past for speaking up, that does not have to be the end of your story, and in fact, it cannot be. Instead, we have to use our voices more powerfully going forward to change not only our fate but an overall system that perpetuates suppression of both men and women, young and old, rich and poor, etc.

Past suppression doesn't have to mean that you can never stand up for yourself again. It means that there was a time you felt powerless, but that time is gone. I know it is challenging to overcome such a situation, but you have to get the life-changing help you need to start standing up for yourself and what you think is right.

Be Engaged

In a 2015 Gallup research study carried out in the United States, it was revealed that only 32% of US employees are engaged in their work, and worldwide, a staggering low of only 13% of employees are engaged. Based on this finding, it is clear that when we are disengaged from our work and our social lives, we quickly become depressed, hopeless, and mentally astray. Some people also blame fatigue and pain as reasons for not being able to shape their lives in ways that are healthy, productive, and positive. As I learned in medical care coaching, "Your body can say what your lips cannot." If you are experiencing chronic pain, illness, or a sense of despair and disappointment that does not go away, you should seek outside help to address the underlying problem.

By facing the roots of the matter, which frequently stem back to your childhood, you may begin to regain your strength, energy and vitality, and sense of self. We all indeed need energy and vitality to craft a positive and meaningful life. We have to stand up and say enough is enough to behavior that we no longer choose to tolerate.

Know Your Worth

In today's world, so many people don't understand or perhaps haven't been taught that they are vitally important, valuable, and needed in the community. They possess exceptional abilities and skills that others would like, and their viewpoints and aptitudes are immensely helpful to others. You have to understand that, once you tap into the process of recognizing and honoring your talents and capabilities and learn how to apply those talents to outcomes that are meaningful to you, you will begin to experience more personal power and become more comfortable exercising it for what you believe in and care about.

Maria Nemeth shared in her book titled The Energy of Money that "we are all happiest when we are demonstrating in physical reality what we know to be true about ourselves, when we are giving form to our Life's Intentions in a way that contributes to others." Based on this quote, are you demonstrating what you know is true about yourself when you are giving form to your life's purpose in a way that is helpful to others in the society? Are you clear about your life's objective, its direction, and the legacy you would like to leave behind when you leave this world?

These questions are critical, and everyone should find an answer to them. You need to start assessing your internal and external power if you want to build a better life. Take time to understand yourself and find out who you really are and what you want in life, and identify more clearly what you will no longer permit. Once you are empowered and strengthened, you will then stop accepting from others what is unacceptable.

Tolerance does not mean you cannot say no to what is unacceptable. It only means that you respond to the situation gently while you look for a permanent solution to the problem. Good citizens always deal with the problem nonviolently, and that is the essence of tolerance.

EIGHT

HARD WORK

"A dream doesn't become a reality through magic;
it takes sweat, determination and hard work."
Colin Powell

IN THE PRECEDING CHAPTER, we discussed the importance and effects of tolerance. In this chapter, we are going to talk about one of the core pillars of a good citizenship, which is none other than work. As you take your time to read, you will come to understand the importance of work and the reason why we work.

Every non-disabled citizen is required to work and to try to add something to the revenues and social funds the country is generating. Since you are very aware that idling is parasitic in the society, we all must work for the welfare of our nation. Work brings in wealth and prosperity in any country. In countries like Russia, work is considered a legal duty for every citizen. This means it is illegal to say you cannot work when you are physically and mentally fit. In criminal law, when something is illegal, it is contrary to or forbidden by law.

Today, work has a fundamental role in the individual's psychological wellbeing and in structuring the meaning they ascribe to their personal life. As an activity, work organizes and provides meaning to the use of time in a society that has programmed its rhythms as a function of work. Work, then, is vital in structuring everyday life and in facilitating continuity.

We have to agree that work has both individual and societal benefits. For individuals, work is considered to be an important activity that structures personal and social identity, family and social bonds, and daily routines, as well as ways of making money. There are stages in life when work is vital. When you are young, for instance, you need to work very hard so that you can rest when you reach the retirement age. You need to work extremely hard when you are under forty, because at sixty-five, you will be retired. For those in the working class, it is believed that work can boost your physical and mental wellbeing, self-confidence, and self-esteem. Psychologists argue that it provides a sense of self-worth, which is directly provided by the feeling that you are contributing to society's common good.

When it comes to society, work is seen as an important feature in promoting community cohesion, increasing civic participation, reducing public spending in a range of welfare, promoting economic development, and organizing social life at a macro level. I want to tell you that if you are doing some work, you must do it honestly and wholeheartedly. Martin Luther King, Jr., once said if a man is called to be a street sweeper, he should sweep streets even as Michelangelo painted, Beethoven composed music, or Shakespeare wrote poetry. He should sweep streets so well that all the hosts of heaven and earth will pause to say, "Here lived a great street sweeper who did his job well."

One may ask what type of work he or she should do. Since independence, South Sudanese have been competing for government posts while ignoring other jobs. Over 90 percent of our working-age citizens see only politics as the most rewarding job, overlooking all other sectors. I know of people who have been hunting for government jobs for years without any success. One of them happened to be a good friend of mine. This gentleman once told me point blank that he would rather stay idle if he didn't find a government job than work in the private sector. This man was jobless for four years until the eruption of the civil war, which ultimately buried his dream as he returned to diaspora where he used to live.

Many people who are not well informed believe in employment while forgetting that they can also work on their own and become employers. It is not a bad idea to look for a job and be an employee, but if that is not available, you cannot waste your time waiting for an unexpected opportunity to come along.

In our society, a man who does not want to work is perceived as lazy. People overlook him, and he does not get any position in a social structure. No one listens to what he says, even if it is good advice that can take the society forward. In some communities, they even find it very difficult to get married because everyone feels that they will be incapable of providing for their families. In other countries, they easily fall out with the law enforcement agencies such as the police, because they tend to cause insecurity by engaging in illicit activities such as drug dealing and other criminalities to prove that an idle mind is surely the devil's workshop. The government does not entertain someone who disturbs the public peace and cannot contribute to the welfare of the country.

At the family level, it is also feared that such people will raise bad children as their kids may follow in their footsteps. In some communities, they are summoned by elders who encourage them to change their habits for the betterment of their homes and the society.

There's a famous Chinese saying which says, "It does not matter if it's a black cat or a white cat as long as it catches mice." I am quoting this saying because, in our society, there are people who do not want to work and give excuses that this work is this, and that work is that, and so forth. This argument cannot help you if you are jobless and have no means of income. You have to take the bad or dirty available job as you search for the clean one. Do not allow people to perceive you as a potential criminal in the society.

Work is also an antidote against boredom and emptiness. Those who are not working are seen as suffering from boredom. When a man is bored, he suffers stress and thinks of committing crimes. Our life is an odd mixture of various moments of action and inaction, work and rest. We have to agree that work provides us with an inner creative joy that saves us from the dullness and boredom of life, as it puts our energies to proper use. Unused energies create disorders in us, making us physically unhealthy and mentally unhappy. When there is no work to do, time hangs heavy on our shoulders, thus making it difficult for us to cope with boredom and stress. This proves that idleness is more tiresome and painful than work.

Work does not only provide us with money that we need to make a living, but it also makes our life meaningful and peaceful. With this, even the most underpaid, unimportant, and unpleasant work is far better than no work.

For us to have instrumental and happy work, we have to do two necessary things: we need skills, and the work needs to be constructive. Many people complaint about constructive work because it is burdensome and unpleasant in the beginning. However, in the end, it becomes delightful if one persists. For deriving maximum predisposition from life, we must view it as a continuous, unified system.

While good work pays and evil work destroys in the end, every man who learns some useful skill can enjoy it until he improves himself completely. This element of constructiveness is an important source of happiness. For example, if you work hard and build up something new for yourself, you feel encouraged and elevated because you have found pleasure from your creative work. When there is no work, there is no joy in life either.

Reasons Why We Work

Human beings are created with purpose, and that purpose is not to sit in tea places or in front of the television for hours and hours while watching endless shows or playing video games. You have to understand that we are meant to work, and we are meant to work for a purpose. Such purposes may include socialization, fulfilling our objectives, or at least getting closer to figuring out what our reason for living might be. Work provides a sense of productivity which is rarely found to such an extent elsewhere. We have to admit that work also improves our standard of living and gives us a platform to revolutionize.

Without work, we cannot escape the rat race and become financially independent or attain financial freedom. If your attitude towards work is more negative at the moment, I challenge you to think of the benefits, because doing nothing or not having a single life goal is meaningless. Work is not only useful but excellent, as it produces the right attitude. It is everyone's goal to be well off financially, and that is the reason why they went to school. No one will ever tell you that he is studying in order to die poor. There is no point in wasting your parents' hard-earned money that they paid for your school fees, only to frustrate them in the end. Let's take a look below at the five reasons why we work.

To Inject Purpose Into Life

Without a doubt, work provides an avenue to fulfill a purpose, or at least the feeling of it. Just getting through each day does not cut it in the long run. As people, we need to have a deeper meaning to life, and work often enables us to fulfill our desires and needs. Many of us today are still struggling to understand why we exist, let alone know why we should work to find our purpose in life. One of the age-old questions that people ask themselves is what their purpose in life is and what life means to them. If your current job is not fulfilling your mission in life, try to explore other untapped talents that you have, and you will find one.

You can do simple things that don't require capital — things like small-scale farming where you plant vegetables for sale. This doesn't require any capital; you only need a hoe to start digging. Within a month's time, you can have your vegetables ready for sale, and you get money. If you are good at fishing, we have the Nile River, which never dries up. Venture into the Nile and start fishing. It will never humiliate you, as you will have your first catch within the first day you spread your net. These activities will help you to garner a sense of accomplishment that only hard work can provide.

It is good to understand that activity precipitates activity. For instance, if you are working hard at your current endeavor, you will increase your odds of running into the next one, which may be the right job that fulfills your life purpose. Purpose does not have to come from your primary career, either. You can be passionate about your family and your extracurricular activities, such as hobbies or serving your community. I want to warn you, do not limit yourself to thinking that your current career has to be your sole purpose in life. That would be a fallacy at best.

To Socialize with Others

Socializing is not the same as socialization, which is the process through which people are taught to be proficient members of society by understanding societal norms and expectations, accept society's beliefs, and be aware of societal values. Socializing is a sociological process that involves interacting with others, like family, friends, relatives, and coworkers.

As a people, we need each other, since we cannot thrive when we do not have a balance of getting support from others and giving support to them. At times, we are depleted, especially when we are only giving but not receiving. I wonder whether you will agree with me that we sometimes get a sense of fulfillment when we help others. Lending a helping hand to friends and family members in times of dire need always strengthens our social network.

Sometimes we work very hard, and we do not have time with our loved ones; thus, we end up depending on social media for interaction. That makes work itself so frustrating and stressful, as it deprives us of the enjoyment that is supposed to come with it. While we have unlimited potential to connect with others on Facebook or WhatsApp, the connection itself is not as influential as having a face-to-face conversation with our dear ones. For us to fill this gap, we have to ensure that we carve out time to connect with those who are important to us at least once in a while. Remember, it does not have to be every day or every week, but maybe you get together with that group of friends or relatives occasionally to catch up on life. This little bit of social interaction could be a catalyst for increasing your work satisfaction over time. If you work alone, find another person that you can share a meal with at least once a week to appreciate the importance of socialization.

To Increase the Productivity of Mind

Oftentimes, there's nothing more satisfying than checking items off your to-do list or leaving a hard day's work feeling satisfied at the amount of stuff you were able to accomplish. For humans, feeling productive is energizing and good for the soul. I wonder whether this could be a blessing of work or a curse. Of course, we are blessed when things go well, and we conclude the day with a feeling that we have accomplished what we had planned for that day. On the other hand, work is considered a curse when we close a day without carrying with us a feeling of productivity due to technical issues, work drama, or other such problems.

To gain a sense of productivity, you need to have a small list of non-negotiable items to accomplish at the beginning of the workday. At the end of each day, you need to outline a few tasks, so that even if nothing else gets done the next day and you achieve these few things, you will feel good that you have won the day. As for the remaining tasks, you have to ensure that you give them the utmost attention the next day.

To Maintain Our Standard of Living

I think keeping a standard of living is at the top of the list of reasons why we work. Of course, we need to work to make money to pay our bills, our children's school fees, rentals, and other expenses. These reasons are evident and valid. In the past, people would not work in the same traditional sense as we do nowadays. Instead, they might have plots of land, grow their food crops, and raise their animals. Not everyone would have the same skills or access to the same provisions, so they would swap or trade their goods or time to get what they needed.

Today, it still works this way, but we are more heavily dependent on actual money to exchange for goods or services. In some parts of the world, some people still make barter trade. Today, there are barter exchange companies based on the traditional concept of bartering goods and services instead of using money.

While work is part of our life, we need to avoid overwork. Many people do not know when to say "enough is enough" as they continue to shoot for making more and more money, which is always done at the expense of their precious time. It is good to work, but consider where your threshold ends and try to maintain a balance of earning and living.

To Enhance Our Creativity

For the last one hundred years, the world has seen rapid technological advancement, as demonstrated by the many innovations we have today. People who were born in the 1940s could confirm this fact and tell you what the world used to look like during their childhood. During those days, there were no computers, smartphones, Skype, or Facebook, among others. In those days, our fathers and grandfathers used to travel far distances on foot. Concerning the mean of transport, those who were considered rich according to their standards were riding on donkeys and horses.

Our effort to work hard has made us to be creative beings. The question is whether we will be able to sustain today's pace of innovation, as that pace seems to be getting faster and faster. Nonetheless, technology today has provided a platform to receive information at an almost instantaneous velocity. This spurs creation and innovation forward. We can continue to build on one another's ideas immediately to make new products, and therefore live better and healthier than before.

We need to work and enhance our creativity, or else we will get stagnant. If you are not doing anything to be creative at the moment, I challenge you to take a step forward and start creating something new.

You have to work by all means, even if it means sleeping on the job. I understand that in most countries, including South Sudan, sleeping at work is considered an embarrassment to the company or organization and it may cost someone a job. However, in Japan, sleeping in the office is widespread and allowed. They consider it as "exhaustion from work," and it is socially acceptable. The Japanese name for this is inemuri, which means "present while sleeping."

Start doing some of the work that will draw you to your career or the area of your life's interest. Work is energizing, as it spurs additional ideas and excitement. With work, we can achieve greatness. Remember, a good citizen is the one who works and contributes something to the welfare of his nation.

NINE

COURAGE

"Courage is resistance to fear, mastery of fear, not absence of fear."
Mark Twain

IN THE PRECEDING CHAPTER, we discussed hard work as one of the important citizenship traits. In this chapter, we will focus on courage, which is also one of the qualities that make up a good citizen. Since time immemorial, people have defined courage partly as the ability to do something that scares them or having strength in the face of pain. Aristotle, the renowned Greek philosopher, believed that "courage is the first of human qualities because it is the quality which guarantees the others."

Most people also see courage as the ability to act on one's beliefs despite danger or disapproval from others. For instance, you can be considered courageous if you defend your religious ideals in the face of threats, if you are a hero who climbs a mountain to save lives, if you lead the fight to make the world a better place for future generations, or if you stand tall against injustice.

One of the best things about courage is that it is completely different for everyone. For some, courage might be physical acts of defiance like running a marathon, while for others, it might be expressing their feelings or standing up for what is right. After all, it takes the same bravery to confront fear.

We are aware that human beings are capable of moving beyond mere goodness toward greatness. Courage allows individuals to try and do the right thing, even if it is difficult or dangerous. That's why Vincent van Gogh once queried, "What would life be if we had no courage to attempt anything?" The answer was "nothing."

Many people — including Benjamin Franklin, Thomas Jefferson, Martin Luther King, Jr., Susan B. Anthony, and Mohandas Gandhi — dared to change the rules to achieve justice. Most of these heroes died gloriously while defending ideals favoring humanity. All these change-makers were driven by courage to contribute to social transformation. As citizens, we have to strengthen our resolve to do the right thing that serves our highest values and the common good.

I understand that it is sometimes challenging for someone to have the audacity to do the right thing, due to the risks involved. However, the right thing doesn't require many to do it. Right is always right even if it's only championed by one person, and wrong remains wrong even if thousands stand in support of it. All that is needed in this regard is a moral courage that rises above apathy and cynicism in our political and socioeconomic systems, as well as across our religious and tribal divides. Today, history still celebrates courageous icons such as Nelson Mandela, Mother Teresa, and Dr. Martin Luther King, Jr., for refusing to back off from pursuing their ideas.

There are those whose daring, sharing, and inventing contribute to our collective future, and for whom culture and democracy are always seen as the beginning point for vision and action. The universal energy of these groups of people gives rise to alternative stories as they embrace the underrepresented while opening up space for learning, living together, and questioning the fundamental nature of democracy.

Courage also means doing things that may be difficult or unpopular to help others. South Sudanese are expected to make wise and ethical choices in their daily lives as courageous people. You may be racing into a burning building to save lives or helping out a person who is being robbed. These are certainly courageous and admirable acts. Even if they are smaller occurrences, they still count as acts of courage.

Courage brings transformation in any country. Without courage, for instance, civil society organizations cannot stand their ground to say no to the malpractices committed by leaders in the society. The fight for corruption, for example, cannot be won if those who want to see the practice change are not courageous enough; the independence of South Sudan could not have been possible if we did not take up arms to say no to marginalization and racial and religious discrimination to liberate our country from our brothers in the north; and your life cannot change if you are not courageous enough to take risks and travel a painful path to discover your destiny. Every good thing always comes with pain and courage.

Courage can be practiced at both individual and group levels. At the individual level, courage enables one to overcome life difficulties. Let's say, for example, you are a graduate today. You might have suffered financial stress that threatened to hinder your success. Whether you want to build a house, start up a business, or engage in farming, you need courage to conquer that fear standing in your way on the path to success. It has been said that whatever you need in life is on the other side of fear. Therefore, courage is a strong weapon to destroy such fear, which has sealed your dream.

At the group level, courage helps society to progress in all aspects. Countries without courageous citizens cannot realize their dreams. In South Sudan, it took SPLA courage to liberate South Sudan from the Sudan. Many heroes died during the twenty-one years of liberation struggle; thousands were killed in the battlefield; some died of both curable and incurable diseases, while others were devoured by wild animals as they trekked to training camps unarmed. Despite all these difficulties, they never gave up the fight against marginalization and Islamization. And because of their courage, we now have a country we call our own.

There is a story about a family of four, including a nine-year-old daughter named Lisa and a five-year-old son, Mark. One day, Lisa was diagnosed with a rare blood disease. The doctors predicted that she would die soon unless they got a cure for the disease, which, according to them, was some amount of blood matching Lisa's, likely to be found in the blood of relatives. All the relatives went to the hospital to be tested. Upon testing, it was found that only Mark's blood was a compatible match with Lisa's.

As a result, little Mark was asked by his parents if he would agree to give blood to his sister Lisa. Without hesitating, he asked his parents if his blood would save Lisa's life. When they said yes, he immediately agreed to give his blood and save his sister's life. Two days later, the blood transfer began. Mark was placed on a bed next to Lisa's until the blood was extracted. After a short moment, he began to feel dizzy and asked the doctors if this was the time he would start dying. The doctors were flabbergasted about why the little boy thought he was dying. However, later on, it occurred to them that Mark never knew the amount of blood required of him to cure Lisa.

As a human being, little Mark might have worried about his fate too for giving out his blood. Above all, as young as he was, he thought that all of his blood was going to be removed to cure his sister and that he would die in the immediate aftermath of the process. As Nelson Mandela once said, "The brave man is not he who does not feel afraid, but he who conquers fear." Mark conquered his fear to rescue his suffering sister. Such is an act of true courage.

As Jean Paul Richter put it, "a timid person is frightened before a danger, a coward during the time, and a courageous person afterward." This was not the case with little Mark. He persevered until the end of the blood transfusion, and above all, he was ready to die. The only difference is that he wanted to know the timing of his death, and that should not be viewed as cowardice for a little hero of five years who sacrificed his blood to save his sister. A coward would not accept such a sacrifice. He would make a lot of calculations and ask countless "if" questions. One of these queries would be "What if the blood that I give fails to cure Lisa's disease?" He may also ask whether both of them could die as a consequence of the blood transfusion and a failure of the blood to cure the disease. Such thinking could have caused stomach cramps and nervousness to a junior citizen like Mark.

True citizens make sacrifices for others to live. Aristotle also stated that "courage involves deliberate choice in the face of painful or fearful circumstances for the sake of a worthy goal." This means there is a close connection between fear and confidence in our daily lives.

We have to put to use a practical framework that integrates the forces of our mind, body, and spirit to make a positive contribution in our society, be it at home, school, work, or place of worship. We have to keep moving and stay motivated, even when we confront obstacles. Bravery isn't always a groundbreaking endeavor. It is a skill that's practiced and honed over time through the small acts that you do on a regular basis.

Types of Courage

You may know about many kinds of courage. However, we will discuss only six types here for the purposes of this chapter: physical courage, social courage, moral courage, spiritual courage, emotional courage, and intellectual courage.

Physical Courage

Physical courage is the type of courage most people think of before they consider other aspects of bravery. Such bravery takes with it all the risks, particularly the risk of bodily harm, which can inflict physical pain and even death on us. In some instances, there are things which we consider more important than fear of pain. For example, you may find yourself running into burning buildings to rescue an elderly person who cannot escape the fire because she is too old to do so, facing an enemy on the battleground as a soldier, climbing a high mountain such as Everest to break the record, or protecting a child from a dangerous animal eager to devour him. These things can only be achieved by people who either have an objective or feel the pain of others.

For them to succeed, physically courageous people always take into account the need to develop physical strength, resilience, endurance, and self-awareness. Pain tells us where our boundaries and limits are, so we should not ignore it. However, some things are more important than pain, and we need to cross the border of our physical fear for a higher purpose.

Our fear of physical pain is often exaggerated when the pain seems more severe in anticipation. In situations like this, dread can become a barrier that keeps us from taking action. To be physically courageous, you need to know that because you participate in the world through your body, keeping it healthy, strong, and resilient prepares you for every kind of challenge.

Social Courage

Most of us are aware of social courage, which involves risks such as unpopularity, embarrassment, or even exclusion. A good example of such embarrassment is what you get from your community when you fail to win a leadership position in the communal election. To confront this and move on, you need to show confidence and keep going with your head held high. Socially courageous people do not conform to the expectations of others if such an expectation is irrelevant. They show their true self despite the risk of disapproval or punishment. You have to express your opinions and preferences without regard for whether they are in line with what everyone else thinks.

When you are wrong, you have to apologize and move on, and that is part of social courage. Social courage is about being comfortable with attention without seeking it out or craving it. You have to ask for what you want or need, and also meet the wants and needs of others. When you are a parent, for instance, it means that you are not comparing your child's achievements with those of another child. If you are a teenager, it means understanding peer pressure and resisting its negative effects. This type of courage often involves assisting others through the development of a charitable mindset.

Moral Courage

Moral courage involves doing the right thing even when it puts ourselves at risk of mistreatment for taking action or speaking out. Hazards associated with this type of courage may include shame, opposition, punishment, or the disapproval of others.

Robert F. Kennedy observed that "few men are willing to brave the disapproval of their fellows, the censure of their colleagues, and the wrath of their society." He also noted, "Moral courage is a rarer commodity than bravery in battle or great intelligence. Yet it is the one essential, vital quality of those who seek to change a world which yields most painfully to change."

Moral courage requires us to rise above the destructive attitudes in our society such as hatred, complacency, and cynicism. Here we tend to enter into ethics and integrity, the resolution to match word and action with values and ideals.

For parents, moral courage often involves setting aside our own momentary wants and desires to set an excellent example for our children and be effective parents. It is not about who we claim to be to our children and others, but who we reveal ourselves to be through our words and actions.

To do the right thing, we must listen to our conscience. If we ignore our conscience, we risk damaging our personal integrity or feeling inadequate or guilty. This type of courage requires us to consider our highest ideals and choose to act in ways that support those ideals. It asks us to recognize that our actions have consequences, whether positive or negative.

Spiritual Courage

Spiritual courage gives us the strength to face deep and challenging questions about faith, purpose, and meaning. For many people, spiritual courage may be rooted in an organized religion, but it can also be developed in non-religious contexts. Spiritual courage implies that we have to be open to the most profound questions about why we are here on earth. Sometimes you find yourself asking difficult questions such as: What is my life for? Why am I here? Do I have a purpose in life?

These profound existential questions can be quite frightening, especially when they involve considering our own mortality, and this helps to explain why so many are attracted to various types of fundamentalism — because we long for definite answers to these questions, we are drawn to beliefs that might seem to provide such answers. But this uncertainty in itself gives us courage that we should never stop asking questions about spiritual matters even though we don't find clear answers to the questions we ask. We should allow ourselves to be vulnerable enough to ask the questions anyway, even if we are unlikely to find the answers.

Intellectual Courage

If you are willing to grapple with the most difficult or confusing concepts and ask questions, if you struggle to gain understanding and risk making mistakes, then you are intellectually courageous. Stephen Hawking, the world's most brilliant theoretical physicist of our time, affirmed this when he defined intelligence as the ability to adapt to change. Intelligence enables humanity to experience and think. It also gives us the cognitive abilities to learn, understand, reason, form concepts, recognize patterns, comprehend ideas, plan, use language to communicate, and solve worldly problems.

Throughout history, the world has proven to be a difficult place for intellectuals to live. People will always question your intellect, doubt your advancement, and challenge you for claiming to be above the society.

Ryuho Okawa, the founder of the "Happy Science" religious movement, wrote that "when the world's usual ways of thinking are opposite to the truth, then the truth will not be accepted, because it is not understood since it does not reflect the common sense of the time." This is an indisputable fact, as we all know that if you happen to be a visionary person who is ahead of your time in terms of thinking, the society may not understand you but only work to misinterpret your visions, because their thinking is so confined to the contemporary world. People are more aware of their contemporaries than what their future holds.

Sometimes what we learn today may challenge commonly accepted ideas, thus contradicting the teachings of our family, society, or cultural group. In the future, intellectual courage will be increasingly required to find new ways of approaching the complex issues of the environment, the economy, and societal challenges.

Intellectual courage may also mean being motivated within yourself to learn and ask questions, rather than needing external motivation. The vastly increased access to information in recent decades has made critical thinking all the more important. There is a Japanese proverb which tells us, "If you believe everything you read, you had better not read." As such, integrity and authenticity are closely linked to intellectual courage. In other words, we are obligated to tell the truth even when it is uncomfortable.

Emotional Courage

Emotional courage means loving yourself and believing in your own self-worth. Self-acceptance is one aspect of emotional courage, and it also involves seeking fulfillment and being willing to move outside your comfort zone. Emotional courage requires us to search within ourselves for the various sources of our concern that can lead to anxiety or depression, and remove those fears from our minds.

This type of courage opens us to feeling the full spectrum of positive emotions at the risk of encountering the negative ones. It is strongly correlated with happiness. The terms "emotions" and "feelings" are often used interchangeably, but they involve different processes:

Emotion is the complex psychophysiological experience combining our internal (biological) response to external (environmental) stimuli. As that emotion crosses the threshold between unconscious to conscious awareness, the verbal and non-verbal language of "feelings" comes into play as we engage higher, prefrontal cortical processes to seek to understand, label, express, suppress, and/or make choices based on the lower and middle brain regions' generation of core emotions. All emotions evoke feelings, but not all feelings evolve from core emotions. Some feelings are subtle variations like ecstasy which is related to joy, or melancholy, which relates to sadness. Other feelings are associated with the states between core emotions and are not directly traced to one core emotion as opposed to another.

For example: let's say there is a loud crashing sound, a stimulus which triggers an emotion. Immediately, the pulse accelerates, the breathing quickens, and a number of other physiological things happen in a cascade without our conscious participation. Then the mind creates a feeling based on thoughts about that stimulus.

(Armstrong and Dungate, 2011).

Researchers have identified a set of core emotions that includes anger, fear, sadness, enjoyment, disgust, surprise, contempt, shame, guilt, embarrassment, and awe. Some are driven by genetic factors, while others are social adaptations. "The most universal are happiness, sadness, anger, fear, and disgust. All are associated with biological intelligence and a drive to survive. Our emotions are an evolutionary adaptation to help support our survival. At a highly unconscious level, the limbic system generates the physical arousal associated with each emotion. Once an emotion intensifies, thoughts begin to form about the emotion, cognition is engaged, and behaviors are generated to deal with the emotion and the needs that must be met. Feelings can help guide us back to the core emotion we are experiencing: they can help answer our need for connection, wellness, and ultimately survival. Emotional intelligence is, in essence, a study and practice devoted to supporting human insight and evolution based on emotional awareness" (Armstrong and Dungate, 2011).

As a good citizen, you need to be courageous. You should possess physical, social, moral, spiritual, emotional and spiritual courage to serve your country better.

TEN

RESISTANCE

"Without strong watchdog institutions, impunity becomes the very foundation upon which systems of corruption are built. And if impunity is not demolished, all efforts to bring an end to corruption are in vain."
Rigoberta Menchú

In the previous chapter, you learned about courage as one of the qualities of citizenship. I believe you now understand the definition of courage, its types, and the importance of each type to you as a good citizen. In this chapter, we will discuss resistance, which is more similar to courage as compared to the other traits of good citizenship found in this book. Topics of discussion contained in this chapter include effects of corruption, corruption as endemic, challenges facing anti-corruption work, the role of community in fighting corruption, and how it can be ended.

If you read the table of contents before you came to this chapter, you may have paused when you saw the term "resistance." You might have wondered what type of resistance this author is talking about and whether it is a violent or non-violent type. This attention might also be driven by a suspicion that you think I am talking about armed rebellion when I tell you to resist.

To be clear, that is not what I intend to preach here in this book, because I do not believe in a bloody type of reform myself. The resistance I am talking about here is a peaceful struggle against malpractices such as bribery, fraud, discrimination, injustice, and other forms of corruption.

Corruption is a disease that requires immediate eradication. It doesn't spare any individual, entity, or country if nothing is done about it. It is often said that where there is war, corruption always thrives. This is demonstrated by the Transparency International report of 2017, which placed the world's conflict-ravaged states at the top of the list of the most corrupt countries worldwide that year.

In its 2017 Corruption Population Index (CPI) report, which was released in February 2018, Transparency International listed Somalia as the most corrupt country in the whole world, with a score of only 9 points out of 100 among the 180 countries assessed for corruption that year. South Sudan was the second in that ranking with a score of 12, and the third on the list was Syria with 14. The other countries in the top ten, all scoring below 20, were Afghanistan, Yemen, Sudan, Libya, North Korea, Venezuela and Iraq. On the opposite end, New Zealand topped the chart with a score of 89 as the world's least corrupt country that year, followed by Denmark with 88 and Finland with 85.

As a true citizen, you have a moral responsibility and duty to say no to any form of malpractice you come across, be it bribery, fraud, injustice, or others. It is your duty as a good citizen to resist injustice from any quarter. If the government at any level is unjust, it is your duty to stand tall and point out the wrong so that it is corrected before it can spread to harm the entire population. If the church is corrupt, the members of the congregation have a right to voice their concern before the faithful run away. If the school is corrupt, the head teacher should be told that school is where knowledge originates and is disseminated, and if it is tainted, the whole nation will be ruined. You have to understand that all countries that progress well have active citizens with high levels of resistance to all forms of malpractices.

While you are working to resist malpractices in your community, you will definitely come across one of the progenies of corruption one day. This type is not new to you, as I have already mentioned above. It is bribery, which is one of the primary means of corruption in most countries in the world. It is used by private parties in both government institutions and the private sector to buy many things. These could include influencing the government's choice of firms to supply goods, services, and works, as well as the terms of their contracts.

A firm may bribe to win a settlement or work to ensure that the contractual breaches are tolerated in its favor. Bribes may also be offered to buy time to speed up the institution's granting of permission to carry out legal activities, such as company registration or construction permits. In the same vein, a company may pay a bribe to obtain a license that conveys an exclusive right, such as a land development concession or the exploitation of a natural resource.

Sometimes, officials may also influence the allocation of government benefits for their interests. These benefits may be in the form of money, such as subsidies to enterprises or individuals or access to pensions. They may also be in-kind benefits such as access to a particular prestigious school, modern medical care, or stakes in private enterprises. A tax collector may also decide to reduce the amount of taxes or other fees collected by the government from private parties as he is being bribed by the taxpayers. When used in court, bribes can change the outcome of the legal process by ignoring illegal activities or favoring one party over another.

In the private sector, fraud and bribery always have costly results. For instance, fraud in an unregulated financial system can undermine savings and deter foreign investment, thus making a country vulnerable to financial crises and economic unpredictability. Banks and other financial institutions may be taken over for fraudulent purposes, eroding trust in those institutions. Small shareholders or savers may withdraw their funds from banks when they learn about insider dealings and the enrichment of managers as a result of weak regulation. When you see these activities happening, it is your duty as a good citizen to take action and save your country.

Effects of Corruption

Corruption is highly endemic in the world, and its prevalence is one of the reasons why many countries are lagging behind developmentally. It is estimated that an amount of US$3.6 trillion is lost to corruption each year, according to the 2018 World Economic Forum. In a speech delivered by UN Secretary-General António Guterres on the International Anti-Corruption Day on December 9, 2018, he underscored that this amount is lost mainly through bribery and theft.

During his visit to Kenya in 2015, President Obama described bribery and a lack of transparency as an impediment to Africa's growth in a continent where 80 percent of the population lives on less than two dollars a day. He urged Kenyans to hold "visible" trials to tackle the problem.

Besides bribery, there are other forms of corruption such as embezzlement, tax evasion, money laundering, and cronyism, just to mention a few. According to Oxfam, it is reported that 30 percent of rich people in Africa hide their wealth offshore purposely to evade tax. This money hidden in safe havens abroad amounts to US$500 billion. As a result, Africa loses US$14 billion in tax revenue every year because the rich few have hidden their money far away from their continent.

Additionally, African Development Bank and Global Financial Integrity found out that up to US$50 billion is lost to illicit financial outflows annually. About 65 percent of this money disappears in commercial transactions by multinational companies.

On the African continent, there is no doubt that one of the factors impeding development progress is none other than unregulated corruption. Unregulated corruption weakens institutions and sometimes leads to their collapse, as funds meant to operationalize these institutions disappear in the hands of a few cliques.

Anton du Plessis, Executive Director of the Institute for Security Studies, underscored that the biggest threat to development and peace in Africa is not terrorism, drought, malaria, or HIV/AIDS, but rampant corruption. It is true that Africa is her own problem when it comes to corruption.

Corruption in Africa leads to lack of opportunities among the youth. Every year, young people from Africa risk their lives to cross the Mediterranean Sea to Europe in search of job opportunities and better living conditions. Many lives are always lost in the international waters whenever a boat capsizes.

In 2018, the International Organization for Migration (IOM) reported the death of 4,503 migrants across the world. Among that number, a majority of them were Africans, as there was no other region that saw as many deaths as the Mediterranean Sea that year. In 2019 alone, IOM recorded a death toll of 363 African migrants trying to cross the Mediterranean Sea to Europe. This is how Africans end up losing their young generation to international waters prematurely because of corruption which, when tackled, could save lives.

When exercised in the private sector, corruption can damage employees' morale in the organizations, as trust is lost in those running the institution. When morale is lost, staff members also underperform, thus leading to the failure of the organization, as it cannot deliver well. The organization's reputation is also damaged, and it will become obsolete in the competitive world. Those funding the organization will develop a low opinion of it or even stop the investment, as no donor dares to support an entity that diverts away resources meant to save humanity. Sometimes, if it survives, there will be increased scrutiny, oversight, and regulation by the bodies that support it.

At the individual level, corruption can lead to termination of an employee. If an employee is facing serious criminal charges, he or she can also be sued in a court of law. Socially, a corrupt person finds it difficult to relate to his family, friends, and colleagues, as he or she can't be trusted with monetary or material things.

Generally, citizens lose confidence in or develop a low opinion of public authorities who cannot deliver services but waste taxpayers' funds. Citizens always lose goods and services when corrupt officials are in charge of their affairs. For example, an international organization or a company may want to implement a project such as borehole or schools but is told to bring the money by the authorities in power. Subsequently, the organizations would shy away from delivering such a service, leading to the community losing the opportunity.

Why Corruption is Endemic in Africa

The reason why corruption is so endemic in Africa, especially in war-torn countries, is the fact that citizens lack civic and political space to express themselves and talk freely about issues affecting their lives. Some of them lack awareness due to illiteracy brought about by persistent conflict, as there is no time for studies.

Where there is active civil war, it is only the gun class that have a say in the running of government. They can influence the policies of the government as it suits them, while non-armed civilians stand by with their mouths shut, waiting for the return of freedom of expression, which sometimes takes ages to come. In this way, the economy deteriorates, currency becomes valueless, and the rate of development decreases further and further since they cannot wait for the return of stability and peace.

Furthermore, the brainpower of the state always diminishes as qualified civil servants flee the country for refuge outside the country's borders. Such an exodus always deprives the country of skilled labor, as those who are left behind become too few to run all the institutions. As a result, some institutions will be dominated by unskilled labor with no idea of where to start, let alone where to go, as they cannot envisage the institution's direction because they have little or no clue about how to run a modern office. When that happens, the institution becomes slack, as there is no headway. All indicators of progress will die, leaving only indicators of stagnation.

Imbalance between the executive branch, the legislature, and the judiciary is another problem that facilitates the prevalence of corruption. In most African countries, the executive organ of the government is always strong, while the legislature and the judiciary are very weak. Their activities are often remote-controlled by the executive body, as they cannot think, make decisions, or execute their mandate independently without the approval of the executive.

In many African countries, the parliament is seen by the masses of people as a rubber stamp for the executive. For instance, if the parliament enacts a law and the law does not please the executive, they will change the law in order to please the executive. They value their relationship with the executive more than they do with the people who elected them to the parliament. This is ironic, as on other continents, the representative of the people would prefer to overhaul or reboot the entire system for the law to take effect.

Another factor that promotes corruption is the absence of nationalism. When citizens lack the spirit of nationalism and allow themselves to be held hostage by ethnic politics, politicians always feel entitled to loot with impunity, as they have protection assurance from their tribesmen. In such an environment, even civil society finds it difficult to operate to advocate for the cause of the civilians, since the general public is divided.

Africans have a tendency to communalize public institutions. When one is appointed as a minister, commissioner, or governor, the whole village and most particularly the individual's relatives and friends will celebrate because their own son or daughter has finally been given a key to the food stores. The home of that politician quickly fills with dwellers as more relatives continue to trace the lineage linking them to the politician. For this reason, it is difficult to criticize an act of corruption committed by such an official, as an attack on an official is viewed as an attack on the entire village and all the politician's relatives. They see him as their own when he is supposed to be a public figure who is entrusted by the nation with the running of the public office. When it comes to appointing workers, the office managers and private secretaries become nephews, nieces, and cousins — people whom he trusts to keep confidential information and stand with him during hard times.

Experts on corruption say that many public officials on the African continent always seek reelection because they see that holding office would give them access to the state's coffers. Some fear justice that may follow after they leave public office. As such, they prefer remaining in power as an indirect way of seeking immunity from prosecution.

Professor PLO Lumumba once said during one of his public lectures at the University of Cape Coast in Ghana that if you want to get rich quick, join African politics. He described African politics as unhygienic because it denies the population the privilege to enjoy their resources, as they are used to enrich the few. As such, he concluded that if a country cannot get its politics right, there is no way it can get its economy right.

Challenges Facing Anti-Corruption Work

The United Nations has instituted a body called the United Nations Convention Against Corruption (UNCAC) as a corruption watchdog. So far, this entity has contributed to establishing new institutions and adopting new anti-corruption policies and legislations in many UN member states. However, there is still a gap between laws, institutions, and policies and their effectiveness to tackle the menace of corruption.

Institutions tasked with oversight responsibility always find it difficult to execute their mandate, as they are sometimes ignored, discouraged, silenced or at worst scrapped by the powerful cliques. One of the bravest and most outstanding anti-corruption workers and activists in the entire African continent is Professor PLO Lumumba of Kenya. During his tenure as the chairperson of the Kenya Anti-Corruption Commission (KACC), Patrick Lumumba made it his duty to educate the masses about the effects of corruption.

He was vocal in his fight against corruption — in most of his seminars, he would refer to corruption as a cancer that has to be eradicated collectively. Shortly after his appointment, he became a televised anti-corruption preacher in Kenya. This angered some politicians who felt that this anti-corruption senior official was running too fast and should slow down. They saw him as a threat that had to be dealt with before he grows horns. As a result, the parliament decided in one of its sessions to pass a law to scrap the KACC, leaving PLO and his team jobless. The disbandment of the KACC was effected on August 24, 2011, during the tenure of President Mwai Kibaki. The commission was later renamed as the Ethics and Anti-Corruption Commission.

After Lumumba was removed, he was interviewed by a journalist who asked him why he had failed to tackle corruption in Kenya when he was heading the Anti-Corruption Commission. He jokingly answered him that it was because he was a lone warrior. After his removal from the office, he disappointed those who thought his fight for corruption would come to an end. Instead, he broadened the scope of his war, as he is now fighting corruption at the level of the African continent as a Pan-Africanist of high caliber.

We live in a continent where big thieves are rewarded with praise and promotion, while small thieves are condemned to death through stoning or burned alive by mobs on the pretext of mob justice. It seems the people who execute mob justice don't know their rights very well, as they prefer to do away with thieves who steal individual items while not being able to touch those who steal public resources. This is a pathetic, illogical, and unfair form of justice.

Africans need to wake up and revolutionize their minds and open their eyes to see the difference. If we cannot take the law in our hands to deal with the big thieves, why should we take the same law into our hands to victimize the tiny thieves? Unless we change this attitude, we will be no different than those we view as corrupt in our midst.

Role of Community in the Fight Against Corruption

In most countries in Africa, many communities are still ignorant, much less claiming what belongs to them. Some do not even have any idea that they have a share in the national cake. However, with the expansion of media and an increase in the activities of civil society organizations in the continent, some rural communities have started to know what belongs to them.

Let me give you a story of one Member of Parliament representing a certain constituency in one of South Sudan's counties who exploited the community's ignorance for years until the community woke up and demanded their rights. This official was given a responsibility to take care of the County Development Fund by his constituents and through the national Parliament. Every quarter of the year when the funds were released, he would disappear with the money without using it for development in the rural area where he comes from. For quite a very long time, there was no single clean water facility, let alone a school or primary health care facility in the area.

One day, the community made up their mind and convened an urgent meeting without his knowledge or involvement. This came after a few intellectuals from the area informed the community about the person who had been messing up their area's development funds. During the meeting, it was agreed that the MP should be summoned to answer some questions on why he was not delivering services to the community while he had been receiving the County Development Fund from the national government in the name of the community.

One fateful afternoon, the elders gained strength, and he was summoned. The elders gathered under a gigantic neem tree, which seemed to be the largest public hall for the community at the level of the rural area. They arranged their sitting stools and some broken chairs, awaiting the arrival of the honorable Member of Parliament, whom some of them wanted to be addressed as a dishonorable Member of Parliament, given his failure to fulfill his duty to deliver the services needed by the community.

He adhered to their request and showed up. The sun was hot that day; the giant honorable member was sweating all over. It was not clear whether the river of sweat was caused by the heat alone or by his fear of confronting the angry elders. Perhaps both. He was given a somewhat clean chair in good condition. The chair was green in color, and it had dark stains on its arms and legs. Although it was a four-legged chair, one of the legs was not strong enough to support the community's representative, who came from capital Juba, where big people like him sit on sofa seats. He lowered himself and sat down more carefully as if he was advised to do so. He greeted the elders, and they responded.

The meeting began. One of the elders, who seemed to be the chair of the meeting, cleared his throat and introduced the topic of discussion. You know Africans are so disciplined. For instance, when they want to farm, they start by digging the bush first.

Before he came to the point, the older man started by telling stories, including how they as elders had worked very hard to convince the community to elect him in a most competitive election. He also shared with him what the community expected of him as their representative in the national government. As he was about to hit the point, he gave him several examples of areas developed by their representatives. He told him that in a certain county not very far from theirs, one of the national Members of Parliament built for his community a primary school using the County Development Funds; in another county, about five water pumps were provided by another hard-working MP in charge of the Community Development Funds. He kept giving example after example. Before he could posit his question, two more elders also spoke and added more examples of community development in other areas he did not mention.

After they gave enough examples of developmental projects, the elder began to explain the purpose of the meeting. "Now that you have heard all the developmental stories in the counties neighboring ours, we want you to tell us where you have been keeping our funds throughout all these years. The floor is yours now."

During his turn, the MP started by clearing his throat noisily like a truck that was stuck in mud while carrying a heavy load of cement. It was not clear whether there was an obstruction in the doorway of his windpipe that threatened to fail his speech, or if he did that to gain fresh energy after the source of his weakness was revealed by the community's mature members.

In about a minute or two, he finished the throat-clearing business and turned to the elders. He started his speech by greeting them as if he had just entered the room. Perhaps it was like a dream to him when the elders gave him a lecture on development programs that he did not expect to come from their mouths. To him, they are mere villagers who could not write or read. Besides, they do not have access to the media. Where do they learn about developmental projects when they have not gone to school themselves? Where do they get that courage to ask the honorable Member of the National Parliament? Someone must have influenced them, he thoughtfully concluded.

He said he appreciated them for calling the meeting. They nodded in acknowledgment. From their response, one could tell that they were more interested to hear the answer to the question they asked than empty appreciation and sweet greetings.

The MP admitted that he had been receiving the Community Development Funds for quite some years. He also acknowledged that he had never delivered any single developmental service to the community. Raising eyebrows among the elders, he told them that he thought nobody knew that he had been messing with the money. "I didn't know that you knew I had been eating your money. Now that you are aware of your rights, I will never touch your money again; I will only use it for the development of the county. Forgive me, and I will not eat your money again," he appealed.

While he was confessing and making revelations, the elders looked at him in amazement. Is it their honorable Member of Parliament making such a revelation? Why should he exploit their ignorance? Is it not his responsibility — and at the same time, the reason they elected him — to enlighten them about the new ways of the world, including its changing colors? They looked at each other in the eyes and gazed at their representative, who sought their forgiveness. There is nothing they could do with a thief of their fund who confessed before the decision-makers of the clan. After all, he promised he would never again misuse the money but use it for the development of the county. They forgave him, and that marked the end of the meeting. From that day forth, the MP changed for good, since he knew that the community was no longer ignorant and blind about his malpractice. Although justice was not served, a slight change in the society was realized after the elders refused to shy away from the honorable Member of the National Parliament.

For a perfect resistance to be realized, all citizens should support anti-corruption commission in fighting all forms of malpractice. For instance, if a customs duty officer stamps and takes from you 1000 SSP, let him or her issue you with a receipt. If he says there is no receipt, insist until he provides one. That money you are giving him is not his money; it is what the government will use later for purchasing medicines for the public hospital and paying the salaries of teachers who are teaching your children in school and the police who are protecting you day and night.

A colleague of mine once shared with me how he perfectly resisted a traffic police officer who wanted to take money from him in an inappropriate way. This particular officer stopped him while he was driving on a highway. With due respect for the authority, he adhered to the traffic rules. As soon as he stopped, the officer approached him. He asked him to roll down the window, which he did. The next thing was a logbook and a driving permit, which he also produced. After he went through these documents, he saw that the documents were correct. Without letting him go, he instead thought of what to do next to penalize the driver. He made up his mind to use speeding as an offense. He told him that the offense he had committed would cost him US$40.

In his response to the police officer, he told him, "There is no problem, as long as you will produce a receipt for that." Upon hearing this, the officer was shocked to encounter a fierce driver. He looked for a better explanation of how he could dodge issuing a receipt. However, he ended up telling the driver that they do not give a receipt for that. In his response, the driver told him that without a receipt, he would not give him the money.

When the officer knew that there was no way out, he decided to let him go. Before he could do that, he asked him for a little money to buy a cigarette. The guy told him that he had begun the process on the wrong footing. He told him that he would not give him anything, and he surely did not. Interesting, right? Do you think this traffic officer would repeat that mistake? I think not, if he has any sense at all. This is how corruption is fought.

Ending Corruption

There is no silver bullet in fighting corruption, as Transparency International humorously put it. Fighting corruption is not one single entity's responsibility. No one can fight corruption alone, not even the head of state, let alone the head of the Anti-Corruption Commission in the country. Fighting corruption is a collective responsibility. It requires the contribution of the press, members of parliament, civil society, civil servants, judiciary, executive, and every citizen in the country.

Education plays a crucial role in eradicating corruption. When the masses of the country are educated, when the rate of literacy is high, citizens tend to know their rights and advocate for their own cause. This awareness increases the rate of transparency, as those who may practice corruption in the name of illiteracy will find it difficult to do so. Resources that would have been looted will be safe, since there is nowhere to hide them, as people are aware of their rights.

Another better way of fighting corruption is transparency in budget allocation. When the budget is allocated, it needs to be publicized such that citizens know how much is allocated and to which institutions. This should not end there; projects implemented with that budget should also be known. It is the role of the civil society organizations, the media, and the general public to follow up on the implementation of these projects.

In addition, there should be tough laws that regulate the rate of corruption. Many countries have strong laws on paper, but they are not implemented by the executive and the judiciary. According to a 2005 survey by the UN Economic Commission for Africa, it was found out that only two countries — Namibia and Malawi — had watchdog groups that were deemed effective by experts. Other countries were found to be ineffective, as the anti-corruption offices were not independent from the executive branch.

Despite these findings, there were a few countries, including Nigeria, that have had some measure of success. For instance, under Nuhu Ribadu as Chairperson of the Anti-Corruption Commission, Nigeria's Economic and Financial Crimes Commission recovered US$5 billion in stolen public funds and secured 250 convictions. In addition, the commission helped pass laws that mandated competitive bidding on government contracts and public audits of the oil revenues sent to state governments. Sometimes, a "naming and shaming" policy works to reduce corruption, as some politicians see this as dangerous to their political careers, since it make them unpopular in the society.

Civil servants, for their part, should play a crucial role in combating corruption in governmental institutions. The same should apply to the private sector. There should be training opportunities to capacitate the workers for better service delivery so that they can better combat corruption.

Additionally, UN member states, working together with international organizations monitoring corruption, the private sector, and civil society, should urgently implement anti-corruption action plans based on UNCAC review recommendations. Should the UN member states fail to adopt such action plans, it will be impossible to eradicate poverty in all its forms and dimensions, including extreme poverty, which the world leaders saw as the greatest global challenge and an indispensable requirement for sustainable development during their declaration of the goals for the 2030 Agenda for Sustainable Development at the UN Headquarters in New York in September 2015.

Fighting corruption, as I have said earlier, is not one person's duty alone. To ensure that the money you paid in the form of tax or in other forms goes to the right people and will be used for the right purpose, we all have to resist any act of corruption. If you do not exercise your duty properly, your child will be charged extra fees by his schoolteacher; you will be insecure from unknown gunmen because the police have relaxed due to lack of motivation. Worse still, you will pay for your medical treatment, since the public hospital has run out of medicine due to your inaction. You have to act now before it is too late.

Tell that tax collector who used to come and collect money from your business without proper receipts that it is not business as usual – "You have to provide a receipt, and I will hand you my money." You have to contribute to state-building by righting the wrong. Think like Nuhu Ribadu, who told Bloomberg Businessweek in an interview in June 2009 that the best way to attack poverty is by attacking corruption. I know resisting malpractice can be challenging when it is done by only a few individuals. However, if all of us do it, corruption could be eradicated and become a thing of the past.

ELEVEN

HONESTY

"Each time you are honest and conduct yourself with honesty,
a success force will drive you toward greater success."
Joseph Sugarman

IN THE PRECEDING CHAPTER, we talked about resistance, which mainly focused on corruption and how we can collectively get rid of it. In this chapter, we will deliberate on honesty, particularly why we should be honest as good citizens.

Honesty is a positive trait associated with such qualities as trustworthiness, integrity, fairness, and sincerity, as well as a lack of negative behaviors like lying, cheating, or theft. Honesty is one of the essential values of good citizenship, as it is a big reason behind the development of any nation. An honest person does not think of hurting anyone through bad habits, activities, or behavior, as they have no appetite to involve themselves in activities that are morally wrong. This is what God advises us in the book of Proverbs in the Old Testament, where it is written:

"There are six things the Lord hates, seven that are detestable to him: haughty eyes, a lying tongue, hands that shed innocent blood, heart that devises wicked schemes, feet that are quick to rush into evil, a false witness who pours out lies and a person who stirs up conflict in the community." — Proverbs 6:16-19

South Sudanese are expected to be honest in their work, leisure, and relationships with others at all times. If we were all dishonest, the rate of corruption, mistrust, criminalities, and chaos would be very high.

As a reminder to you, if you are a civil servant working in the oil industry, for instance, know that you are there because the public has given you their full trust. They expect you to keep the track record of barrels produced or sold each day. If you are in the banking industry, the public trusts you with their million pounds or dollars because you are one of their own; they do not expect you to grow extra teeth to harm them. It is not an easy task to serve the public. If you cannot be honest, you'd better quit and do your own things instead of claiming to serve the public. In traditional Africa, anything connected with the public is always feared because the public is a hodgepodge of people with different degrees of powers and innumerable beliefs. If the spiritual leaders call on divine powers for whatever reason, the village has to prepare for good or for ill, depending on the reason. As diverse as they are, they have powerful demigods that you could not imagine.

In the Holy Bible (Acts chapter 5), we have heard of the story of Ananias and his wife, Sapphira. Ananias sold a piece of land belonging to the church with the full consent of his wife. He kept back a part of the cash for himself, but brought the remaining amount and placed it at the apostles' feet. When Peter saw the money, he found that the money was far too little. He therefore said to Ananias, "How is it that Satan has so filled your heart that you have lied to the Holy Spirit and have kept for yourself some of the money you received for the land? Didn't it belong to you before it was sold? And when it was sold, wasn't the money at your disposal? What prompted you to think of doing such a thing? You have not lied just to human beings but to God."

No sooner had Ananias heard this than he fell down and died. In the aftermath, great fear seized all those who heard what had transpired. Some young men came forward, wrapped up his body, and took him out and buried him.

Nearly three hours later, his wife appeared, not knowing what had occurred. At that moment, Peter asked her, "Can you tell me whether this could be the precise worth you and your husband Ananias got when you sold the property?" "Yes," she replied, "that is the price." Peter said to her, "How could you contrive to test the Spirit of the Lord? Listen! The feet of the men who took away and buried your husband are at the door, and they will carry you out too." At that moment, she fell at Peter's feet and died instantly.

When the young men came back and found her dead, they again carried her out and buried her beside her husband. At that time, great fear seized the entire church and all who heard about these events.

Integrity is a great wealth you have never heard about. There is a famous story about an honest man called Tom Smith, a civil servant serving his government. Though he was poor, he earned much respect from the society he served. When he was about to die, he called his children and gave them his last advice. The advice was simple: he told them to follow his footsteps so that they could have peace of mind in all that they do. One of his children, a girl by the name of Sarah, defied his advice. Instead of mourning as her father was about to die, she instead told him, "Daddy, it's unfortunate you are dying without a penny in your bank. Other fathers who you used to label as corrupt or thieves of public funds left houses and properties for their children. Look, even the house we live in is a rented apartment. Sorry, I can't imitate you. Just go, and we will chart our course."

A few moments later, their father gave up the spirit. They continued to hustle after their father's death. Three years later, Sarah Smith was shortlisted for an interview in a multinational company, and she went. Inside the interview room, the chairman of the committee asked her, "Which Smith are you?" She replied, "I am Sarah Smith, daughter of the late Tom Smith." The chairman cut off the interview and yelled, "Oh my God, you are Tom Smith's daughter?"

He turned to the other members of the interview panel and said, "This Smith man was the one who signed my membership form into the Institute of Administrators, and his recommendation earned me my place here today. He did all this for free. I did not even know his address; he never knew me. He just did it for me."

He then turned to Sarah and said, "I have no questions for you anymore. Consider yourself as having gotten this job. Come tomorrow, and your letter of appointment will be waiting for you."

When Sarah Smith came the following day, she was made the company's Corporate Affairs Manager, and she was given two cars with drivers, a duplex attached to the office, and a salary of £1,000,000 per month excluding allowances and other costs.

After Sarah had worked at the company for two years, the Managing Director of the company came from America to announce that he intended to resign and needed a replacement. A personality with high integrity was sought after. In the end, the company's consultant again nominated Sarah Smith to the position of Managing Director.

In an interview, she was asked about the secret to her success. With tears in her eyes, she replied, "My daddy paved the way for me. It was after he died that I knew that he was financially poor but highly rich in integrity, discipline, and honesty."

She was asked again why she was weeping, since she is no longer so young as to miss her dad still after a long time. She replied, "When he was preparing to die, I affronted him for being an honest man of integrity, but I think he can now forgive me as he continues to rest in his grave. I did not work for all these. He all did it for me, and I only walked in."

So, finally, she was asked whether she would follow her father's footsteps as the late Tom Smith requested. Her easy answer was, "I now adore the man, and I have a giant picture of him in my living room and at the entrance of my house. He deserves whatever I have after God."

From this short story, you can see that if you are a civil servant, it is essential to be like Tom Smith in all that you do, to leave a good heritage for your children after you are long gone. It pays to build a name; the reward does not come quickly, but it will come, however long it may take, and it lasts longer. It is said that integrity, discipline, self-control, and fear of God make a man wealthy, not the fat bank account or the number of villas you have.

Many leaders know that honesty and integrity are the foundations of any leadership. In most parts of the world, leaders stand up for what they believe in. Jon Huntsman, Sr., the multi-billionaire who started a chemical company from scratch and grew it into a US$12 billion enterprise, wrote in his book, *Winners Never Cheat,* that there are no moral shortcuts in the game of business or life. Mr. Huntsman classified people into three kinds. To him, the world is made of unsuccessful, temporarily successful, and those who become and remain successful in life. He considers character as the quality that makes such a difference among these categories of people.

True honesty can help you pass a job interview even when you didn't get all the answers right. The current Google CEO Sundar Pichai went through that in 2004 when he was first interviewed at the company for the position of Vice President (VP) of Product Management. He was asked by the interviewers whether he had seen Gmail. There were two problems here. First of all, the day he was interviewed was April 1, 2004, exactly the same day the Gmail service was announced, and he had never heard about it, let alone seen it. Second, the fact that it was April 1, "April Fool's Day," made him think that the question was a joke.

In his answer, he was honest and said no. This won him the trust of the interviewers because he was intellectually humble and honest enough to admit that he knew nothing about the new service, which was just introduced in the market that day. When he was shown how to use the service later, he was able to give a correct answer to the question.

If he had attempted to create his own answer to that question, he would have lost the opportunity to get the position. Many companies and employers value honesty and intellectual humility over lies. They don't entertain those who are not honest with themselves and with others.

Great leaders never compromise their honesty and integrity by opting to cheat. That is what integrity means. Integrity means doing the right thing because it is the right thing to do in itself. True leaders of honesty and integrity may not be famous or flashy, but they do not care or compromise their values for cheap fame. They are fond of keeping their promises. When it comes to promises, they give promises carefully and sometimes reluctantly, because once they make a promise, they follow through on that promise without fail. In whatever you do or whatever decision you make, you have to be frank, and that will make you effective. Wise leaders are careful not to surround themselves with yes-men who will only say what they want to hear instead of telling the truth.

Sometimes we need to ask ourselves this daring question: Have you ever imagined what could happen if all the people in this world became dishonest for even a single day? I think there could be more corruption even in broad daylight. People would work only to make money, and they wouldn't think about the social responsibilities, teamwork, or goals of the institutions they are working for. In a situation without ethics in business, the gap between the poor and the rich widens, as the poor become poorer and the rich become richer.

There would be no long-lasting relationships or friendships, but more court cases, police work, crimes, and violent activities in the society. There would also be more stress because of doubts in relationships and friendships, as well as in business dealings. Again, if leaders are dishonest, they will only think about themselves and their profits without thinking about developmental activities or other people's welfare.

We know very well that not all people are honest, and not all are dishonest. You and I also know that most people do not care about honesty and truthfulness in today's selfish world. Most of those who are dishonest are unable to understand that dishonesty creates problems for them in their later life. Some also hardly realize that the problems they are facing today are a result of their dishonesty and dealings in the past.

Why Honesty is Important

I have already talked about how important it is to be an honest person, although I will have to emphasize it once more time. Without honesty, there would be no foundation for any lasting or pleasurable relationship in any context, whether at the family level, with friends and neighbors, or in the community. Honesty is a voice for love and a strong pillar that builds trust and faith. In the absence of it, even the phrase "I love you" can be nothing but a bucket of a lies, as there can be no real security in the relationship.

At some point, almost all of us have been hurt while we interact with others. Such hurt may come in the form of a revealed secret, a distorted truth, a fabricated lie, or a discovery of something that should have been talked about openly. Dishonesty hurts because it jeopardizes the relationship, creates doubts, robs trust, and brings about unnecessary stress and paranoia. Being honest is not always easy; otherwise, we would all do it all the time.

Being honest does not just mean telling the truth about factual information, but also about the way you're feeling. If you were hurt by something that someone did to you and you do not raise the issue with them, they may never realize how harmful it is unless you are honest with them and tell them how you are affected. However, if instead, you hide the way you feel, then you disempower the other person from doing something about the problem and deny the relationship an opportunity to grow. They may also feel hurt if they realize you were upset with them but said nothing, or if they know you're not honest with them about the way you feel. All of this festers and damages the relationship, whereas being honest concerning your feelings will bring healing, solve problems, renew hope, and foster sensible communication.

Sometimes when people do not know the truth, they will try and do guesswork in an attempt to dig out the truth of the matter. Lack of honesty always makes people try to figure out what we are not saying to find out what the truth is. This sometimes breeds gossip, which can then foster more lies and deception that other people may mistake as the truth about us. However, when the truth is finally out, many more people feel hurt and betrayed, all of which could be avoided if honesty had been applied in the first instance.

People are usually hurt by the concealment of the truth more than by the truth itself. Some people lie because they are afraid the truth will get them in trouble or cause another pain. While the reality could also be painful, it is still typically less painful when delivered honestly than when it is wrapped in deception. Holding back on that or lying to hide it solely causes people to feel betrayed as well as hurt.

Honesty has some social benefits. One of them is the fact that it improves the relationship and saves us from having to live a lie. Living a lie is hard work, as it means not being yourself or enjoying relationships, which is not comfortable for anyone. While being honest about difficult situations may be uncomfortable at first, it is the only way to strengthen a relationship, build trust, and deepen love.

Honesty is an important part not only of our everyday life as private citizens but also in business and the operation of governmental institutions.

According to the behavioraleconomics.com website, a study was carried out in 2016 to investigate honesty, beliefs about honesty, and economic growth in fifteen countries, and a large cross-national difference was revealed in relation to the economic development of nations. The results showed that average honesty was directly related to gross domestic product per capita, suggesting a relationship between honesty and economic development. Wherever you go, people tend to believe that, without honesty, the safety of a country's resources from those in charge of them is not guaranteed.

Honesty is also important at the family level. One way to practice it is to talk to your children about what it means to be honest and why honesty is an important value. This may mean encouraging them to build trusting relationships with one another and helping them to develop self-awareness. The moment they know the importance of being able to trust one another, let them also acknowledge that telling the truth may seem difficult, as we sometimes do not even notice when we are lying. As a parent, you should emphasize to your child that lying is wrong. However, it is also important to note that there are occasionally good reasons to lie or not tell the entire truth, and provide specific examples. For instance, if your child is given a gift that he does not really like, do not let him say "I do not like the gift." Let him say "Thank you." The phrase "thank you" will conceal his feelings instead of showing a gloomy face that could expose his disapproval of the gift.

In whatever we do as grown-ups or elders, let us not forget that children learn values by watching our actions and the actions of other adults they respect. Whatever behavior or habit you portray, they will copy it and put it into practice. For instance, if you are a parent who is violent at times, your children will also be violent. If you are peaceful, your children will learn to be peaceful too. A child acts according to what he sees from his parent. To avoid imparting negative behavior or bad habits, you have to pay close attention and see whether you are modeling honesty and integrity in your day-to-day dealing with your children, or if you are modeling dishonesty. Take notice of whatever you are doing. When your actions do not align with the messages you are sending, you need to adjust them quickly. We all know that nobody is one hundred percent perfect, but each one of us has a responsibility to improve his honesty level for the benefit of his children.

Honesty in School

Academic dishonesty has also become a major concern among school-aged children, including university students everywhere. In a 1992 survey targeting 15,000 at thirty-one top universities in the United States, it was found that academic dishonesty is a real concern, as 87 percent of students in engineering, business, science, and humanities were found cheating. In order to address this, it is important to adopt strict measures capable of disciplining those found to be involved in dishonesty whenever such behavior is reported or detected. Doing so will promote the quality of education and allow for fair competition among the students and morale-boosting.

In addition to student dishonesty, teachers are often blamed for their own dishonest habits by students. In any school, you will also find at least one teacher, or perhaps two or more, favoring some students at the expense of others in the class. Such favoritism may come in the form of marks awarded during the exam. When I was in primary six in the year 1996, I faced this problem with one of my school teachers. It was during the third term's exam, when I happened to be the class's highest-performing student. After we were all given our examination results, we calculated our marks, and all my classmates found out that I had scored the highest marks in the class.

During those days in my district, Leer, there was a system of reading out the top ten pupils' names during the parade, although they awarded only the best three students. However, this was not done immediately after the exam but during the reopening of the school in the following term. As usual, we were allowed to go for our holiday for three months. When we came back the following term, it was announced that the ceremony would take place within that first week.

One fateful morning three days after the opening of the school, a big parade was convened. All the pupils who knew that they had performed very well were smiling. Even without asking, you could distinguish between the smiles of a mere top ten pupil and a top three pupil. Smiles were bright as the sun as expectations were very high, especially among those who knew they were there to reap what they had sown. I was among the most excited ones on that day. I was an enchanting young boy in a dark blue crisscross suit wearing a smile of primary six's best-performing student of the final term.

The school principal and all the teachers sat facing the school ground, which was filled with all the primary pupils ranging from primary one to primary seven (as there was no primary eight yet). They started calling the top ten of class seven, and all seemed to have gone well. After class seven, I knew that it was coming to my class, primary six. I was certain that it would start with me. I began to wind up, imaging how I would majestically walk to the high table to greet the well-dressed education masters and eventually take my gift. However, things did not turn out the way I imagined.

My class master, an energetic medium-sized young man, stood up with the list of well-performing pupils in his hand. He moved to the podium with his chin facing the southeastern direction of the playground, exactly where I was standing. I could imagine how he scanned our eyes from row to row, knowing before he could speak that something fishy was going to happen. After a while, he exhaled and started to call the names in ascending order.

All of my classmates were looking at me in anticipation, expecting that my name would be called instantly. Unfortunately, when the teacher read out the names, my colleague, who was known to be number two by everybody, became the top pupil, and I was called number two. It was a drama. I felt like the world was tearing apart. I broke down and became unconscious. All my classmates fell very sorry and even became very angry about this unfairness. When I regained some strength, I was told to go to the podium and pick my gift. I refused to go. Immediately, I could see from his eyes that the teacher also felt guilty as his energy declined. The school administration also sympathized with me.

When the investigation was done a day later, it was found out that he gave my colleague who also performed very well three extra marks so that he would lead me by one mark, even though we all knew that he was behind me by two marks. The following year, I became reluctant in my studies because I lost trust in that teacher. I presumed that even if I worked hard, he would still discourage me. This forced me to leave the country and continue my education abroad.

From my story, you will see that dishonesty among teachers is disastrous, as it kills the student's spirit quickly. It reduces their commitment to their studies, as they feel that whatever they do will be a waste of time since the results are already predetermined. For this reason, and for the benefit of the nation, the government needs to be watchful for any dishonesty committed by teachers.

TWELVE

COMPASSION

*"The purpose of human life is to serve, and to show compassion
and the will to help others."*
Albert Schweitzer

In chapter eleven, you learned about honesty and its importance
to good citizenship. You also understood why honesty is crucial in
our schools for the learning of our children and of ourselves. In this
chapter, we are going to discuss compassion, how to achieve it, and
why it's crucial to be compassionate as a good citizen.

Compassion is the emotion that you feel when you genuinely care
for other people and other living things, as well as the universe. In
different terms, it means "to suffer together." Emotion researchers
define it as the feeling that arises when you are confronted with another
person's suffering and feel motivated to relieve it. In Hinduism, it
means having kindness, feeling other people's pain and suffering, and
avoiding harming others for one's own purposes. In that religion, it is
one of the twelve most important virtues.

Compassion blooms in a person who rises above his own selfish
desires and appreciates the virtue in others. A compassionate person
is sensitive to the problems, feelings, and emotions of others. As such,
he does not take advantage of their weakness, criticize them, or make

them feel guilt or shame. He shows kindness because he is well aware of the evil in the world.

Unfortunately, this important character trait is fading away gradually on our watch in today's world. Not many have a desire to internalize and experience the inner souls of other people in the hope of helping them.

Some people mistake compassion for other traits such as empathy. Compassion is not identical to empathy, though the ideas are inter-related. Empathy is just the ability to understand or psychically read another person's thoughts, feelings, and emotions without doing much to help the situation. However, compassion enables us to think about others and see the importance of their needs. You have heard of philan-thropists who donate millions; neighbors who share the little they have with their neighbors to ensure their kids do not go to bed with empty stomachs; and bosses who support their staff morally, materially, and financially when they have lost loved ones.

Biblically, compassion is one of the traits that can qualify a Christian for heaven. I repeat, "one of the traits." Many saints traveled this path for them to be remembered in the book of life. If you are a Christian, I believe you have come across the story of Giovanni Bernardone, better known as St. Francis of Assisi.

In the year 1206, Giovanni Bernardone, the son of a wealthy merchant, was twenty-three years old when he decided to go on a pilgrimage to St. Peter's Basilica in Rome. Upon his arrival in Rome, he could not help but notice the contrast between the opulence of the basilica and the poverty of the beggars sitting outside. Wanting to learn from the beggars, he persuaded one of them to exchange clothes with him. He gave his nice clothing to one of the beggars, and he was given dirty clothing, which he wore. He spent the rest of the day in rags begging for alms.

This experience was a turning point in his life. After the pilgrimage, he founded a religious order for those who would work for the poor and the lepers. The brothers in the order also gave up their possessions to live in poverty like those they served. This was one of the first great empathy experiments in human history.

Today, Giovanni Bernardone, alias St. Francis of Assisi, is remembered by Christians for declaring, "Grant me the treasure of sublime poverty: permit the distinctive sign of our order to be that it does not possess anything of its own beneath the sun, for the glory of your name, and that it have no other patrimony than begging." Francis is also known as the patron saint of animals and nature because of his way of seeing God through all things created, which led him to address every created being as his brother or sister.

In the recent past, researchers have ranked nations by the empathy of their people. According to data collected from 104,365 adults across 63 different countries as posted on the sciencealert.com website in 2016, it was discovered that Ecuador was the most empathetic country in the world, followed by Saudi Arabia and Peru.

As a true citizen who cares about his nation, including its contents, you must be compassionate. When I talk about the contents, I mean every living being, including animals inside the territory of South Sudan. As selegnior citizens, we have a role in educating junior citizens, such as children, in loving others in the society. When we cultivate tenderheartedness in our children, we are indirectly contributing to the social development of this nation. Compassion can help positively guide their actions and behaviors.

Compassion is paramount in our society. The assistance you give, no matter how little it is, may go a long way in solving the problem it is meant to solve. You may not be paid back monetarily, but the smiles you will get out of happiness of the ones assisted is beyond financial reward. Not only that, such a smile could bind you together as one people.

Compassion has a power that is stronger than empathy because it is about imagining the suffering of others at a deeper level. Consequently, it is more likely to motivate action. One thing you may not know about compassion is its benefit to oneself. As other people benefit from you materially and emotionally, you as a compassionate person also benefit psychologically and spiritually, since it has proven and remarkable psychological effects on the one who practices compassion.

Such benefits may include relief from depression and anxiety, which you always get when you are happy. You have to understand that when we focus on alleviating others' suffering, we alleviate our own in the process too. As humans, we are always happy when people smile at us, when others render us support and when we are appreciated for what we do better.

In ancient Bulgaria, there was a classic story that children listened to from their parents before going to bed at night. This story was meant to cultivate a sense of compassion in children as they grow up. At that time, there lived an older man in a small village behind a mountain. This man lost his wife early in life, and all he had left was his one and only son. The boy grew up and married a good woman he loved so much. After the marriage, the young family settled to live within the family house along with the father. God blessed them with a son of their own, and soon after that, another. All of them lived happily and peacefully in the house. After some time, the home started to get too crowded, as it became too small for the family.

As time went by, the older adult was getting ill and became expensive to take care of. He couldn't bring wood for the fire any longer or sell the fruits of the farming land at the markets. He was always around, and the young wife slowly started resenting him. After a few months, the young woman couldn't bear living around, cleaning, and feeding the older man anymore. She said to her husband, "Either the old man goes, or I go and take my boys with me!"

The son's heart became heavy with the burden of the choice while figuring out what to do. Most of the time, he would feel restless in the bed even after his wife was sleeping calm and deep at night. For many days, he developed a habit where he could look neither his father nor his wife in the eye.

One morning, he told his older son and his sick father that they should go and collect some wood from the further side of the forest, as the woods on the nearer side were so wet that they could not burn. "I can't go alone," he told them. "Come with me, both of you. Take your walking stick, or you can't make it that far," he said to his father.

They prepared vigorously as the three of them left on the path leading to the remote forest. As they reached the door, he kissed his wife, and he promised her that his father would not come back home with them when they returned. When they reached the far end of the forest and sat on the green grass to eat some lunch, the older man was already tired. He was so exhausted, and he fell asleep within seconds.

"Get up my son, we're going back now," said the little boy's father.

"Yes, Father, let me wake up my grandfather," responded the little boy.

"No, don't wake him, let him sleep. Let's just go. We can get wood closer to home on our way back; no need to carry it from here," said the little boy's father.

"But is he going to find the way back home? Won't he wonder where we went?" inquired the little boy.

"Your grandfather is an old man now; he needn't come back with us. We can leave him here; he isn't needed anymore," said the little boy's father with a heavy heart and the image of his happy wife in his mind.

Father and son had not even lost the older man from sight when the boy suddenly ran back to where his grandfather was sleeping. Before his father could say anything, the boy came back while carrying his grandfather's walking stick, which was by his side where he was asleep. Upon seeing the stick, he told his son, "We don't need this anymore, son! Leave it with the old man and come."

"No, father," said the little boy. "In fact, we don't need it now, but when you get old, and we don't need you anymore, I don't want to have to carry you all the way here. Instead, I will give you this walking stick so that you can just walk yourself until you reach this side of the forest."

Upon hearing this statement, a tear dropped from the man's eye, and he began to cry. As a result, he took the walking stick from his son's hands and ran back to his father to wake him. The three of them slowly walked back home. From there, he told his wife what happened, and they both agreed that the older man should stay with them. From that day on, the old man was honored, loved, and cherished until his time came to leave this world.

In the Mosaic Laws, we are told that anything which you consider hurtful to you, you should not do it to others. In this story, the man expects his son to treat him well when he grows old, yet he does not want to treat the old father in the way he wants to be treated. In the New Testament, we are also told, Do to others as you would have them do to you" (Luke 6:31). So, whatever we do to others, it will be done to us in the same way.

How to Be Compassionate

For you to be a more compassionate person, you need to practice experiential empathy in many ways. Below are some of the things you must do for you to be considered a compassionate person in society.

Anti-Poverty Campaign

One way to practice compassion is to take part in an anti-poverty campaign, since thousands of people each year live below the poverty line. You can do that on social media or during social gatherings. I always used to say that the world is full of resources and everything that humanity needs. There are people blessed with material and financial resources, but these people sometimes feel that they are too busy to lend a hand to the suffering people. They have to be reminded by you, who have a clear idea of how to beckon the sleeping lion. As a good citizen, you have a responsibility to organize fundraising campaigns and help the poor with the money collected. You can buy food or non-food items with the money you raise to assist the needy.

Another structure that sometimes needs to be reminded is the government. If the government is busy attending to other things that are less urgent, tell them how their subjects are languishing on their watch.

Do Volunteer Work

I talk about volunteering in most parts of this book. Volunteering is the sole responsibility and important role of any citizen who wants to be good. You may be preoccupied with other work; however, when you are on holiday or enjoying your weekend, you need to spare some hours each day and spend time volunteering in social development activities. Such activities can range from serving as a schoolteacher at a local school in your village to coaching the youth on life skills. This contribution can go a long way in changing the society.

Attend Different Religious Services

Many of the problems we have are due to the fact that we see ourselves along religious lines. This perception has killed our sense of compassion. We have decided to make our circles small by showing sympathy to people who belong to our faith before we go to the outside world. This is true in our world today — when there is a civil war in a Muslim nation, Muslims will show utmost solidarity to their fellow brothers who share the same faith before they lend a supporting hand to a Christian nation whose civilians share the similar plight. It is the same with Christians, too, and those of other faiths.

If you believe in a particular religion, you need to spend a month or two attending the services of different religions. I tried this myself while working as field staff for the United Nations. As a Christian Catholic, I had always had a low opinion of sharing the mass with other denominations, let alone other religions. One particular Sunday, I happened to join a consortium of denominations, including the Muslims. All were praying in one place. The mass was led by a young Ghanaian military officer, who doubled as a master of ceremonies that day. There was a slot for songs, and I found myself singing aloud as if I were a member of the choirs in that church. The Muslims who were there sang the Christian songs too. You could not differentiate who was a Muslim and who was not as we all sprang up to sing songs of joy.

After we finished, the master of ceremonies asked us to sit down. It was now time to read the holy books. The first slot was given to a young armed officer who read from the Quran, and another soldier was also given a chance to read from the Bible. Once they finished, the master of ceremonies called upon the imam to preach on the Quran. A young, energetic Ghanaian imam, about one and a half meters tall, who was seated at the right front row of the church, stood up. From the way he walked to the stage, there was no doubt that he was energetic and full of life. He wore a broad smile at the corners of his mouth as he addressed the faithful. He introduced the theme of the day according to the Quran. At first, he talked about the prophet Mohamed's early life and how he grew up from childhood when he was a shepherd, including how he met his partner.

After a lengthy preaching, he switched to Jesus. He mentioned how Jesus was born of the Virgin Mary and raised by Joseph. He also talked about Abraham and how God answered his prayers, blessing him and his wife Sarah with a baby boy by the name of Isaac when they were hopeless about fertility as an aged couple. I was touched by his teaching. Without knowing what I was doing, I found myself recording his powerful preaching with my smartphone.

When he finished, he went and sat down. There was a moment of applause in the room as everybody found themselves clapping for this gentleman. After he finished, an Anglican priest went to the podium to preach. As he stood, he acknowledged that the young imam had covered all the topics as he taught about both Mohamed and Jesus. He didn't waste much time; he only said a few points, then returned to his seat. From that day, I stopped being negative about Islam.

For us to be truly compassionate, we need to understand other religions, stop stereotyping, and attend interfaith prayer services, including forums and meetings of humanists. Doing so will rekindle the humanity in us so that we think about the poor and the disadvantaged without drawing religious lines.

Visit Slums and Hunger-Stricken Areas

One of our problems is that we confine ourselves to our comfort zones. More will go amiss if we do not acquaint ourselves with the real world where poverty lives. Most governments often fail to recognize the rights of the urban poor or to think of incorporating them into urban planning, thereby contributing to the growth of slums. This is because they believe that if they provide public services to the poor, it will attract urbanization and cause the slums to grow.

If you are in town, you have to make an effort to visit the areas of your city that you always hear of as poverty-stricken areas. If you see the suffering children, you will feel their pain and fulfill your godly responsibility of helping the poor. You do not have to be a millionaire to help others. You help others with what you have, be it in your mind or in your hand. It is your responsibility.

Fast

Fasting is understood as a person's willingness to abstain from food or drink, or even both, for some time. When abstinence from all food and liquid continues for a defined period, it is referred to as absolute fasting or dry fasting. In Christianity, there is a strong biblical basis for fasting, particularly during the forty days of Lent, leading to the celebration of Easter. Jesus, as part of his spiritual preparation, went into the wilderness and fasted for forty days and forty nights, according to the Gospels. In the Holy Bible, fasting is abstinence from food, drink, sleep, or sex to focus on a period of spiritual growth. Specifically, we tend to humbly deny something of the flesh to glorify God, enhance our spirit, and go deeper in our prayer life.

In Islam, there is a particular season called the season of fasting, with thirty calendar days allocated for this purpose every year. Fasting during the holy month of Ramadan is one of the five pillars of Islam that additionally embody prayer and charity. To fast, Muslims abstain from eating, drinking, smoking, and engaging in sexual activity from dawn to dusk. They follow the lunar calendar, which means Ramadan arrives several days earlier each year. To them, fasting teaches the believer self-control because it disciplines their desire or need to drink or eat during the fasting period. Moreover, it makes any Muslim strengthen their beliefs and be closer to God, making them more blessed and happier to be with God and to serve Him.

Christian fasting and Muslim fasting share the same desire, as the two faiths tangibly demonstrate that God is even more ultimate than the gifts of creation. In general terms, the practice is almost the same, though the two styles of fasting are different. While Christian fasting is rooted in the completed work of Christ Jesus, who purchased God's acceptance for His people by submitting himself unto death, Muslim fasting, on the other hand, represents a longing for approval through the demonstration of submission.

These days are not meant for fasting, per se. They were set by the Islamic and Christian religious scholars to remind followers of both faiths about the suffering of the poor. Doing so every year reminds them about the plight of humanity everywhere in the world. Throughout my life, I have learned that an empty stomach is a good mathematician, quicker to find a solution to any problem than a full one. If you think I am riding on your back, take a look at the world's greatest entrepreneurs. Most of them will tell you they suffered at an early age before they became well off. It is our responsibility to learn to suffer in order to help others and fulfill our humanistic obligations.

THIRTEEN

RESPECT

"Treat people the way you want to be treated. Talk to people the way you want to be talked to. Respect is earned, not given."
Hussein Nishah

IN CHAPTER THIRTEEN, we discussed compassion, how to achieve it, and why it's crucial to be compassionate as a citizen. In this chapter, we are going to focus on respect, its different types, and why it's critical as a citizen to be respectful.

Respect is a positive feeling as well as an action shown towards someone or something considered important or held in high esteem or regard. It expresses a sense of awe for decent or valuable qualities. Respect often comes as the result of a learning process. This is because most people learn how to respect others as they work very hard not to discriminate or to do actions that may offend others. In your day-to-day life, you need to greet and speak to others in a kind and respectful manner whenever you come into contact with them. If you are on a public bus, for example, consider giving up your seat to the elderly, sick people, or pregnant women if you happen to be on board with them. Every one of us wants to be treated with respect. As such, we should treat others with respect, as we would like them to treat us in return.

At times, one finds it difficult to respect others. Some of us are selective in choosing whom we should respect and whom we should not. Egotistic humans rarely respect others, but they demand that trait from others. They would tell you that you do not have respect, although they know very well that it is lacking in their own heart. Others respect only those superior to them while undermining those they consider inferior. For instance, one may respect his boss but not his subordinate. That is completely wrong because respect is neither a one-way street nor selective; it is a two-way street and multifaceted in nature.

Respect for self and others is an essential citizenship quality. Self-respect allows us to take pride in our behavior and our work. Again, respect for others ensures that every one of us genuinely feels a part of South Sudan. It also means valuing different ideas and perspectives. We must treat people with respect if we want to have a meaningful and positive relationship with others in our society.

Being respectful toward other people is a key aspect in life for successfully forming and maintaining positive relationships. If you treat people with kindness, they will also be kind to you. Like charity, respect also begins at home and then spreads to the neighborhood.

If you are a child, you have to begin by respecting your parents and elders, especially your father and your mother. At the same time, you should treat your brothers and sisters, both young and old, with respect too. If your respect for your parents and elders is low, I have a touching short story that might completely change your attitude.

Many years ago, there was a frail older man who, in his old age, went to live with his son, daughter-in-law, and a four-year-old grandson. As old as he was, his hands trembled, and he could not hold a plate or cup properly without shaking. The older man also had blurred eyesight and faltered step due to old age. His son, daughter-in-law, and grandson always used to eat together with him at the same dining table. After some time, the elderly grandfather's shaky hands and failing sight made eating difficult for the rest of the family. Peas used to roll off his spoon onto the floor, and he was having difficulties in holding the glass too. Whenever he grasped the glass, milk would spill on the tablecloth.

One day, the son and daughter-in-law became irritated with the mess he had been causing during dinner. The son said to his wife that they must do something about the father. "I have had enough of his spilled milk, noisy eating, and food on the floor all the time." That fateful evening, they decided to isolate the older adult by setting aside a small table at the corner of the dining hall. The grandfather ate alone while the rest of the family enjoyed dinner together.

Since the grandfather had trembling hands, he broke the dish twice on two different dates. This continuous breaking of dishes angered his son and daughter-in-law, and they had to think of additional punitive measures against the older adult.

Having given up, they decided to serve his food in a wooden bowl, which they made. The older man remained isolated for some days. Whenever the family glanced in the direction of where he was eating, sometimes they would see tears in his eyes as he sat alone. Despite such tears, the only words the couple had for him were sharp admonitions whenever he dropped a fork or spilled food.

The four-year-old boy was always there to observe the situation but had nothing he could do other than to remain silent. One evening before supper, he was playing with wood scraps on the floor. His father noticed him making a wooden plate similar to the one his parents used to feed his grandfather. He asked his son, sweetly, "What are you making?" Just as sweetly, the boy responded to him, "Oh, I am making a little bowl for you and Mama to eat your food in when I grow up." The four-year-old boy smiled and went back to his work.

These words struck the parents so hard, and they became speechless. Immediately, tears started to stream down their cheeks as they cried. Though no word was spoken, both knew what must be done to reverse the situation. That evening, the husband took Grandfather's hand and gently led him back to the family dining table. For the rest of his life, he ate every meal with the family, and no one dared to talk harshly to him ever again. Moreover, for some reason, neither husband nor wife seemed to care any longer when a fork was dropped, milk was spilled, or the tablecloth was soiled.

The moral lesson of this story is that whatever you do to others, know that it will also happen to you. Imagine if the two spouses mistreated their aged father, and they did not want to be mistreated by their son when they grow old. If God had not warned them through the little boy's action, the older man would have died a miserable death caused by stress, loneliness, and grief.

When you honor someone by exhibiting care, concern, or consideration for their needs or feelings, you are already a respectful person. We need to accept others for who they are, even when they are different from us or we do not agree with them. Our country is made up of sixty-four tribes. For it to become a nation, we need to respect our differences by embracing each other. Such respect for differences is what we call "respect of diversity." We cannot only respect our own tribesmen and we say we are one nation.

Before you finish this chapter, I also want to make sure you do not confuse respect with fear. Fear and respect are completely different things. People can fear you and abide by what you say when you are present. However, when you are not there, they will do their own things. To understand what I am telling you better, you need to read this short story.

A long time ago, there was a ruthless king by the name of Virat Singh. His Majesty King Virat was a ruler of the city of Vijay Nagar in South Asia. His reign was characterized by cruelty. All citizens were fearful because of his leadership style, which had no sympathy for humanity. Like many kings who like pets, Mr. Singh had a dog which he called Jack. He loved this dog more than anything in his kingdom. Life was good, and everybody, including Jack, was happy.

One fateful morning, that all changed. Something was wrong with the King's pet — Jack failed to wake up that morning. Later on, it was confirmed beyond all doubts by the servants, including the King himself, that Jack had passed on. As wealthy, caring, and loving as he was, the King organized a historic last ritual for his dog. When he announced the ritual day, the entire city came to the cremation ground to attend it. The place was so congested to the extent that no one could move his foot, as there was no empty space left unoccupied. Eyewitnesses said that even Jesus Christ's death did not attract such mourners when he was killed.

When he saw a huge attendance at his palace, he was pleased to see that people loved him so much, and he felt he was the most popular King in the world. But this turned out to be a misconception of the truth. The ritual was over, and everybody left the venue.

A few days later, Virat Singh, the cruel and highly feared King, succumbed to sudden sickness and died. The city was silent like a windless lake in the middle of the night. No one came to his funerals because he used to be cruel to them during his life. They had to humiliate him, although he was no more. They believed that his spirit would feel the shame wherever it was in hell or heaven above.

If people could attend a dog's funeral and cannot come for yours, then there is a fundamental error in your life. There is a thin line between fear and respect, which every one of us should understand and make the necessary corrections before it is too late. Respect is something you have to earn, as you cannot force others to respect you. As for fear, never attempt to make people fear you, because it is not a good human value.

Respect is also fundamental in our workplaces today. The era of globalization has made respect an important value every worker should possess at the workplace, as we now work with diverse people from different nations, races, and religious backgrounds around the world. Having a diverse workplace is very important because it helps boost our productivity as we learn from each other.

Among coworkers, there must be respect to enhance diversity and reduce job-related stress. Another way of keeping respect at the workplace is politeness. We need to be polite with each other, stop judging people, control our anger, and inspire others to do more. Practicing humility, respecting other people's time, and trying to be empathic are also important variables at the workplace.

Types of Respect

You will see that the list below is somewhat long, as there are many types of respect. However, the most crucial thing is self-respect. If you achieve respect for yourself, you can easily succeed in having respect for others, for social norms, for nature, for values, for laws, for culture, for the family, for national symbols, and above all, for human beings.

Respect for Self

When we talk of respect for self, we mean respect for oneself. John Rawls, an American political philosopher, argued that "a just society must provide the social bases of self-respect for all citizens, for, without self-respect, their lives are severely diminished." He believed that each reasonable citizen has his or her own view about God and life, right and wrong, good and bad.

To be precise, this kind of respect refers to the ability of human beings to respect themselves while being aware of their self-worth. In your life, including in whatever you do, you need to value and appreciate yourself regardless of your condition and shape. However, such appreciation is only realized when a person has confidence and self-esteem to accept oneself irrespective of what others think of them.

Respect for Others

This second type of respect refers to our ability to tolerate, accept, and consider other people regardless of our differences with them. Sometimes, we are tempted to disrespect others when their viewpoints differ from ours. This is why we call for tolerance and perseverance. We also need to respect our parents, men and women alike, teachers, older and young, those whose faith differs from ours, and people of different racial backgrounds. Being respectful of others is very important if we want to become better people. It goes beyond treating others with good manners and listening to them while acknowledging differences in a friendly way.

It is also important to be respectful of other people's time, ideas, experiences, and lifestyles. By showing respect, we acknowledge others and recognize the importance of treating them with integrity. Respecting others does not mean you have to praise them or agree with their opinions. No, that's not it. You have a right to disagree with someone, but in a more respectful manner. If you do this while treating the other person with dignity, you set the example for how you expect to be treated in return. To be precise, the golden rule for respect for others is to "treat others the same way you would want them to treat you."

Respect for Social Norms

The third category of respect refers to the ability of people to respect all the norms that govern their society. Social norms, or customs, are the unwritten rules of behavior that are considered acceptable in a particular society. Their function is to provide order and predictability in our society, since people always want approval as well as belonging. The few who do not follow the norms sometimes suffer disapproval or are considered outcasts by the community.

Societies are kept functioning not only by direct rules but also by expectations. It is believed that when people know what is expected of them, they tend to comply. Despite the application of social norms, there are still some people who seek to be different. Norms can change according to the environment, situation, and culture within which they are found. However, when they change, people's behavior will also change accordingly. Such change or modification may occur rapidly or over a period of time. Rapid change always suffers resistance from the community, since everyone possesses the fear of the unknown.

In South Sudan, every community has a good number of norms governing their existence. These include the rules of courteous behavior or social etiquette, such as observing the official working hours, respecting other people's belongings, letting others speak without interruption, and respecting others' opinions. In churches, meeting places, and public settings in general, we are expected to put our phones on silent mode to avoid interrupting the event.

Young people are expected to be kind to the elderly by doing little things, such as opening a door or giving up a seat. When dining, it is against the societal norms to talk with food in your mouth. You are also expected to chew with your mouth closed and avoid making loud sounds while eating. In some countries, you can be required to pay fines if you spit or pick your nose in public. Even when you want to sneeze, you should say "excuse me."

Respect for Nature

Respect for nature refers to the appreciation and conservation of the environment. There must be environmental and ethical principles capable of regulating the moral relations between humans and the natural world when showing respect to nature. In his book titled Respect for Nature: A Theory of Environmental Ethics, Paul W. Taylor says the ethical principles governing those relations determine our duties, obligations, and responsibilities with regard to the Earth's natural environment and all the animals and plants that inhabit it.

Taylor is of a belief that "every organism, species population, and community of life has a good of its own which moral agents can intentionally further or damage by their actions." According to him, "to say that an entity has a good of its own is simply to say that, without reference to any other entity, it can be benefited or harmed."

We have to respect the universe with all its contents such as animals, plants, rivers, and others. For us to do this, we must desist from throwing garbage into rivers or fields, cutting our forests unnecessarily, mistreating nature, wasting water, harming animals or insects or fields, tearing up plants, or mistreating nature and using environmentally unfriendly practices.

Respect for Family

Family is the first institution in human society. All those who are members of associations, unions, corporations, organizations, or governments today started with family membership. All the people elected to positions of leadership who have respect for humanity today came from families that value respect as a life requirement. If you see a good doctor, engineer, or teacher, to name a few, just know that they were brought up with respect in their respective families.

The book of Sirach in the Holy Bible tells us that children are required to respect their parents. In that book, it is written that whoever honors his father atones for sins, and whoever glorifies his mother is like one who lays up treasure. The same book says that if you glorify your father, you will have long life.

In the book of Colossians, wives are told to submit themselves to their husbands, while husbands are told to love their wives whole-heartedly. They are also told to treat their wives in a respectful manner and avoid being harsh to them. Any family that does these things is always a blessing to the society. If children respect their parents, if wives are humble to their husbands, and if husbands love their wives and are not harsh to them, respect in the family always thrives.

Respect for family is one of the most important types of human values. It implies being able to understand and respect each other within the family. It also put into consideration our ability to comply with a set of rules regulating our coexistence at the family level. Sometimes the guidelines for respect are clear. In most cases, they can just be spoken out loud, shared, and demonstrated. Sometimes, these guidelines are silently in place to follow and to honor. In many settings, family members are allowed to ask questions about what is expected of them, including their participation in setting those guidelines.

Open communication should be key to thrashing out paranoia and mistrust, which are always brought about by a lack of communication. Members of a family ought to be honest, straightforward, and trustworthy with one another. If communication and trust happen between members of the family on a daily basis, it makes establishing the family rules for respect much easier.

Family members know when they are being respected, and they know when they are practicing respect in return. This is because each family member is unique and has his or her own style and personality to live their life. For us to be able to respect strangers, we have to start showing such values at home. Researchers believe that most of the world's problems are created by people whose parents fail to fulfill their parental role in the children's upbringing.

Respect for Values

I used to say that a human being is lifeless when they are stripped of their values. Life in us blooms better when other people value our worth. For this reason, this kind of respect refers to our ability to honor our own principles, which always constitute our self-worth.

People, organizations, or companies might proudly share their core values with you. However, the best way to identify these values is to watch how they behave, because some people, companies, and/or organizations do not match what they say with what they do. For instance, a tobacco company may not be consistent with its core values of caring for consumers or the general public, since they emphasize profits over public health.

One thing I like about tobacco companies is that they are honest with their advertisements. They will honestly tell you that "tobacco kills." When you buy it and die of its effect, that will be your business and not theirs, since they have already warned you. You cannot sue them in any court of law in the world because they have been frank with you by warning you about the dangers of the tobacco prior to smoking. Of course, not many companies will advertise negative core values, but you can judge what really lies at the heart of a business's mission by examining how they act.

A core value is only true if it has an active influence, and if the people or company manage to live by it, at least most of the time. We must recognize that core values are not always consciously chosen but may be instilled by one's parents and community at any stage in life. In every society, the elderly pass on values of good conduct to their children. This means all of us were taught moral principles, ethics, moral code, moral values, moral standards, code of behavior, standards of behavior, and rules of conduct when we were young by our parents. For this reason, if you find bad elements in the community, it is not because the community did not teach them how they should be good people; it is simply because in every market, there must be a mad man.

Everyone should be aware of their own values and live by them. Some people already live by strong core values without realizing it. For you to know what your core values are, in case you do not know, ask yourself what activities bring you the most joy in your life. You also want to know what activities you could not live without.

One may ask a question such as "What gives my life meaning?" or "What would I like to achieve in my lifetime?" If we can articulate answers to these questions, I am sure we will likely see a pattern that can be traced back to a single concept, such as having a consistently positive attitude or using our creative thinking to improve the world. Knowing your value is in itself a strength.

Respect for Culture

Respect for culture refers to the recognition, protection, and continued advancement of the inherent rights, cultures, and traditions of other people. The ability to recognize that there are other beliefs we should respect as humans, even if we do not follow them ourselves, brings us together as one people. The problem we have with culture is that when people think about it, their first thoughts go either to race or to ethnicity. We have to understand that culture goes far beyond that. Our cultural orientations are influenced by other aspects such as gender, class, physical and mental abilities, sexual orientation, religious and spiritual beliefs, age, and much more. In reality, we are all members of various cultural groups, and our cultural identities develop based on the influence of these attachments.

We should not need to have a homogenous culture to be one people; unity of purpose can also happen in heterogeneous societies with different cultures. Like most things that make us who we are, the development of our cultural identity is an ongoing process. If we are exposed to different sets of beliefs and values, it may not be difficult to adapt to other cultural beliefs that were not part of our original makeup, since the culture is dynamic and complex.

Some examples of this kind of respect would be refusing to impose our beliefs on others when they are not ready to receive them. In traditional Africa, for example, superstition is still very high, and a good number of people and societies are still following that path. If you are not superstitious, do not attempt to abuse their belief, because doing so will only create religious schism. You need to avoid making judgments about the opinions of others unless they ask you to do so.

Respect for National Symbols

National symbols are those patriotic symbols representing the national people, goals, values, or history of different nations around the world. Even ethnic groups that do not have their own country can sometimes use these symbols for various purposes, since they serve as unifying factors for the people. Respect for national symbols refers to the ability of the citizens to value and appreciate what they stand for. In any country, good citizens are required to show full respect for national symbols because of what they represent as well as the message they send.

Every country has its own symbols, although there are also common symbols that they share. In South Sudan, our national symbols are the national anthem, national flag, coat of arms, public seal, medals,

South Sudan Pound (SSP), festivals, and commemorations of state. Our pledge of allegiance and national anthem deserve the honor and respect for the ideals they represent. However, our citizens are not living up to these ideals, as some have forgotten that our problems are caused by us and not by our symbols.

Cynthia Miller-Idriss (2016) writes, "National symbols everywhere deserve respect not because they are static representations of unchanging ideals, but because they offer a focal point for diverse societies to express and navigate what it is that unites and represents them." Symbols help us to understand the world around us as the basis for our judgments. We also use symbols to identify with one another and take part in society together.

Some countries have more national symbols than others do. For instance, in India, in addition to the common national symbols, there are other symbols such as the national animal, national bird, national flower, national tree, national fruit, and national vegetable known as Kaddu, which they also call Indian Pumpkin. Although it looks like a pumpkin, it has the taste and texture of butternut squash.

Respect for Human Beings

This is an overarching consideration which represents recognition of each human being's intrinsic value. In this regard, human beings have the opportunity to exercise autonomy and make their own decisions without interference from others. Such exercise of rights should be within the confines of the law that prohibits us from stepping on other people's feet.

People who show this type of respect always have the ability to comply with legal norms or laws protecting humanity. We also need to familiarize ourselves with a bill of rights regulating the right to life, such that we value other people's lives without doing them harm. These rights are stipulated into our Constitution, which is the supreme law of the land.

Importance of Respect

Respect is an import trait of good citizenship, so allow me to reiterate it again. Without it, our relationships with others, especially the interpersonal type, can be irrefutably conflicting and dissatisfied. This is true because if we don't respect others, they will surely hesitate to give us their respect in return, since respect is universally known to be reciprocal.

In this way, being respectful to others, being respected, and respecting ourselves increases our self-esteem, self-efficacy, mental health, and wellbeing. More importantly, it is essential to feel safe and be able to express ourselves without fear of being judged, humiliated, or discriminated against.

FOURTEEN

DISCIPLINE

"All successes begin with self-discipline. It starts with you."
Dwayne "The Rock" Johnson

IN THE PREVIOUS CHAPTER, you learned about respect, its different types, and why it's significant as a citizen to be respectful. In this chapter, we are going to discuss the significance of discipline and where to apply it.

Discipline is understood as the ability to manage one's feelings and overcome one's weaknesses. It is an assertion of resolution over one's basic wants, and it can also be thought of self-control. Self-discipline is the most cherished habit, practice, philosophy, and way of living everywhere, as it has brought about control to the world that would have suffered at the hands of anarchists. The term comes from the Latin word discipulus, meaning "to learn." In contemporary societies, the word "discipline," has a different connotation, as we usually think about punishment for wrongdoing when we hear the word. However, this is not always the case, as discipline can also be voluntary, although there are situations where it can be imposed on people. Institutions such as primary schools and military training camps are known for the imposition of discipline.

A disciplined person is one who has the willpower to overcome any condition or situation he or she comes across. Willpower is good, as it enables us to save for the future rather than splurge everything unnecessarily. In school, it is that commitment and resilience that makes us keep our heads down to study and work hard to earn our degrees even when we really don't feel like persevering with the challenging school life. It also enables us to be bold and say no to that tempting second bottle of beer, cigarettes, and all forms of illicit drugs. Failure of self-control is disastrous, as it can sabotage all the goals we have in life.

Discipline involves taking initiative to get started and having the resilience to hang on. Being a disciplined person gives you the strength to face physical, emotional, or mental challenges. Self-discipline also includes the ability to control one's own thoughts and actions. For instance, a child's ability to delay gratification is an essential element of self-discipline. All successful men and women in history, including the ones we see in our society today, are highly disciplined in the vital work that they do. Moreover, all great successes in life are preceded by long, sustained periods of focused effort on a single goal and the most crucial target, with the determination to stay with it until it is complete.

Throughout history, we find that every man or woman who achieved anything worthwhile and lasting had engaged in long, often unappreciated hours, weeks, months, and even years of intense focus and disciplined work in a particular area. No man can achieve a goal without a sense of discipline. For us to reach our full potential, we need to develop self-discipline in our daily lives. We must also show restraint in our workplaces and other critical institutional structures of the land.

Discipline of Goals

Foremost, the discipline of goals requires us to sit down with a note pad and a pen and take the time to think through and write down all the things we want to accomplish in the next one, two, three, four, five, or even ten years. When we are doing this, we have to organize the list into various areas of our life starting from our family, our health, our career, our money, and other aspects that are essential to us. After we do that, the next step is to set priorities among our goals and rewrite our lists so that our most critical goals appear at the top. We then have to take a separate sheet of paper and make a list of all the things that we can think of doing at the moment to move us toward the attainment of our most important goals we set for the future.

Life is about planning. If you don't plan for your life, circumstances will plan it for you. However, it will be disastrous if you choose the latter. Circumstances are not good planners. They can transform you into an addicted football fan, drug abuser, and/or notorious gambler.

If you decide to watch football or do any other non-beneficial activity during your leisure time, let it not interfere with your reading timetable, work, or business. Remember, anything that makes you abandon your work and delay your plans is detrimental to your life and future.

I have been telling friends and relatives that football leagues are like the River Nile that flows from eternity to eternity with no sign of stopping. When people tell me they are watching football to waste time, I sometimes give them a look of amusement because I know time cannot be wasted. Time instead wastes people who do not know how valuable it is. If you want to watch the football, do it for entertainment and mental refreshment, but with limited and planned time.

Self-discipline begins with the mastery of our thoughts, and if we do not control what we think, we cannot control what we do either. Nevertheless, the good news is that it is something that we can learn by continuous practice over time until we master it. There is virtually no goal that we cannot accomplish and no task that we cannot complete if we have mastered the ability to delay gratification, because we will have the ability to discipline ourselves to keep our attention focused on the essential task in front of us.

Discipline in the Workplace

The sole purpose of workplace discipline is to alert employees of their behaviors and actions and help them understand how these inhibit performance and productivity. Discipline in the workplace is significant for the growth of any organization or company, anywhere in the world. However, it is not always perceived that way by some employees, who feel uncomfortable with the set rules regulating the conduct of the workers. For this reason, almost every employer has been in a situation where he realizes that he has a problematic employee who needs to be disciplined.

Sometimes, the manager or the employer might be tempted to overlook the problem to avoid disrupting the peace. They might also be tempted to overreact out of anger and frustration when the situation seems to be unbearable. However, the good news is that experts on human resources have pointed out that the best way to administer discipline in the workplace, since this issue should never be ignored, is by conducting a one-to-one, private interaction that concentrates on behavior. Many studies have affirmed that properly administered discipline in the workplace helps a business stay away from several common problems, as it helps the company or an institution in a number of ways.

When disciplinary actions or rules in a workplace are clear and transparent, when they are enforced consistently, and when they apply equally to every employee, many employees always behave in a manner that supports the growth of the company. Yet despite the clarity of the rules, some employees may still view them negatively. Many employees would say companies and organizations use discipline policies to justify firing people, but that is not the only purpose of discipline in the workplace; other reasons may include instructing employees in proper procedure or making decisions about internal promotion. Disciplinary review and corrective action help companies to apply the guidelines written in employee handbooks or other documents.

Disciplinary review helps to identify employees who engage in toxic behavior in the workplace and to correct these behaviors in a timely manner. Corrective measures will be applied to employees who deliberately disregard policies and procedures, and they may be among the first to be laid off if the company needs to downsize. Though a sacked employee may complain, an employer's disciplinary policy helps to justify actions to remove staff with toxic behavior from the workplace, as employees who engage in conduct that runs afoul of the organization's philosophy are first subjected to disciplinary action and then face ultimate dismissal. Finally, these measures help employers see where employees' workplace actions may conflict with the organization's philosophy and mission.

Discipline in the Family

One of the most important types of discipline, the mother of all disciplines, is the one found at the level of the family. Discipline in the family is critical, especially for the upbringing of children. When we say discipline begins at home, it means we stock our families with enough discipline before we extend it to the outside world. A family that lacks this vital aspect of life has no clear life direction. Children will grow up without respect for their elders if they are not trained to respect their parents at a tender age. Such children will not be able to take responsibility or fulfill their obligations as parents when they reach parental age. Sometimes they grow up while engaging in criminal activities. They can become gangs and robbers on your watch and frustrate the future you aspire for them to have.

Children who are not disciplined also have no time for God, as they will be busy fulfilling the satanic mission. Once they surpass the tender age, they will always defy their parents' orders and instructions. Parents are advised to instill discipline in children once they start talking. In my opinion, the best age to educate a child is between one to eight years. At this age, the child still believes in you as a guardian. At the age of nine or ten, they will start to get exposed to outside influences. If you do not put enough into a child's mind at a young age, it is likely that the child will adopt only the advice or real-life situations he sees or learns from outside the family.

In disciplining children, parents have different approaches and styles of child upbringing. First, there is a category of parents who treat children like a bottle of ghee and do not want to make their kids unhappy. They claim to be loving them to such an extent that they can't shout at them or beat them when they make mistakes. These parents do not make any effort to correct their children even if one of them insults or slaps a visitor. They think it is normal. Children who are brought up this way grow up thinking that whatever they do is perfect.

These same children will have a problem with their parents later on in life. They like a happy and comfortable life, yet they do not want to do hard work. They do not even care about the parents who claimed to have loved them and treated them like princes or princesses. If they fail to get what they want in life, they easily venture into illicit activities such as drug dealing and other criminalities.

Another category of parents are those who give birth to children they do not take care of. This group of parents marry and reproduce because their age-mates are also married and have kids. They do not know exactly what it means to be a father or a mother. Children born to these types of parents grow up without a sense of love and care, as they are neglected. There is no love and care being shown to them at a juvenile and carefree age. To make matters worse, their parents do not even bother to discipline them or provide for their childhood needs. The children grow up this way, seeing themselves as parentless, as they are no different from orphans. When they grow up, they are forced to discover a world of their own and choose who they become.

These children can also do well if they are brought up by good Samaritans such as nuns and clergymen. However, if they choose a path of crime, they become merciless robbers and terrible criminals.

The third type of upbringing is the one that involves the use of force by the parents. Parents, in this case, use the stick as a tool of correction. They demand a lot of discipline from their children. Every time a child makes a mistake, he will be given a punishment that makes up for the mistake he did. This parenting style is good but can be dangerous for the psychological health of a child when it is done excessively or when smacking is involved. Overdoing it is also harmful to a child's physical health. Sometimes a child will tell a parent to the face that he hates him or her for brutalizing him.

This method of beating a child can be successful or unsuccessful. It is unsuccessful when a parent beats a child but does not explain the reason why he or she is being beaten. The effect of the child's mistake on his or her future life needs to be explained to him. This method can also be unsuccessful if the parent doesn't have a sense of love for a child. If you don't provide for his or her needs and you keep beating the child whenever he or she makes a mistake, the child will grow to hate you.

However, this method can be used successfully if you beat the child moderately, such as giving him or her a few lashes, and you summon him for a counsel thereafter. You should already be trusted by the child, in the sense that you love him or her and the child knows it. The child also knows that you will provide for his or her needs.

I know some parents would say that if you provide everything that a child asks for, it will be disastrous for him or her, as you will spoil the child. I would not say you are wrong or right. You may not provide everything that a child asks for, but if you can afford it, you can provide what he or she likes the most. If you do this, then in most cases, the child will grow to remember you positively for the rest of his or her life. Such children will also inculcate the same spirit in their children once they become parents.

The last category of parents are those who use dialogue instead of beating to discipline their children. This style is mainly adapted by religious parents who see inflicting physical harm on children as a sin before God. They show maximum love and great care to their children. However, if a child errs, they summon him or her and provide counsel. This can work for children between the age of four and eight. As for those from one to three years of age, you can only shout and warn them from doing things that are considered bad. This is the style I am currently using with my children, and I do not know how it will turn out.

Discipline in children is crucially important. In the Holy Bible, the scripture says:

> "Fathers, do not exasperate your children; instead, bring them up in the training and instruction of the Lord." — Ephesians 6:4

The Bible says that parents who choose to care for and discipline their children truly love them and are following the Lord's command. If we inculcate discipline in our junior citizens at a tender age, we will also have senior citizens capable of providing for the nation in the future.

Importance of Discipline in Schools

Every good performance in school can be attributed to discipline. Disciplined students know how to organize their time to study and do every assignment given to them by their teachers. It also helps them complete their exam preparation and homework on time, and enables them to gain the highest score. Those who excel in school also earn more respect from their colleagues. In every school, education masters set rules and regulations that enable the progress of school learning and enhance quality human relationships between the students and teachers.

In any country, the central aim of school discipline is unquestionably the safeguarding of order, safety, and the harmonious work of education within the classroom. Without discipline, teachers would find it difficult to maintain order and respect among the students, as the students could be disheartened and stressed, thus killing the educational quality. Eventually, this could lead to failure to fulfill the goals and objectives of the education.

Discipline in school is sometimes associated with norms. Its imposition in some schools, on the other hand, may be motivated by other non-academic goals, usually moral. Many societies with strong religious roots sometimes emphasize a palpable religious ethic and impose a discipline that goes beyond the classroom. Such norms may come in the form of mandatory attendance to religious services, participation in sports, mealtimes, the formation of a structure of authority within the home, strict management of sleep time, an official system for the request of exit permits or visits, and many other such cases.

These rules outside the schoolroom are obligatory, and in most cases, they come with corporal punishment, especially in the case of minors. In the most extreme circumstances, if students fail to stick to the rules, it leads to the loss of certain privileges, including expulsion from the school.

Teachers have authority and should not use it abusively, but through it, present their ideas, knowledge, and experience without disrespecting the students. They should instead encourage them to participate actively in all school activities. Teachers should also put forth challenges that require students' action and interpersonal exchange with a view toward reflection and discussion, and jointly identify remedies for challenges encountered in the education journey. It is also important for both teachers and students to understand that discipline is not the same as forced rigidity, which can lead to an unsuccessful result in the end.

It is also crucially important to teach the students that whatever is presented in the classroom should also be reviewed at home, to have a greater retention of the content. Doubts can be highlighted when necessary. However, they can always be clarified later if there is no time in the class.

In education, discipline is very important. Many believe that without learning discipline, education itself is incomplete. Discipline helps students to listen to teachings well and also to cover the entire syllabus in the classroom. With it, students are able to wake up early and get ready to go to school on time. It is also believed that discipline in schools helps students to stay healthy, which is good for the growth of both body and mind.

Discipline in the Military

Discipline is a crucial part of military training, as soldiers develop self-control and competence so they can follow important regulations. In a letter to his Virginia Regiment Captains in the year 1757, Lieutenant Colonel George Washington described discipline as "the soul of an army," which "makes small numbers formidable; procures success to the weak; and esteem to all." This demonstrates that military discipline is also seen as a state of order and obedience that solidifies the chain of command.

Soldiers who have discipline always do the right things without being told by their officers. They take full control and responsibility in everything they do even in the absence of the commander.

Discipline is created within a unit by instilling a sense of confidence and responsibility in each member of the army. During wartime, discipline serves as the code of conduct the army follows in its operations. Because of discipline, members of the military do not leak information about military operations to the public. Such confidentiality is crucial and beneficial to both military forces and civilians.

Role of Discipline in Civil-Military Relations

Discipline is essential for civil-military relations in any country because it enables the two groups to define their boundaries and understand their roles in the society. Without discipline, civil authorities across the world can find it difficult to rule over the members of the military who operate the tanks, warplanes, missiles, chemical weapons, and other types of weaponry. Below are some reasons why discipline in the relations between the military members and the civilians is so important.

Promoting Peace and National Integration

For peace and national integrity to prevail in any country, there must be discipline among the military members and the civil population. Such discipline enables a harmonious relationship between the military members and the civilians. For instance, in the United States, the Department of the Army within the Department of Defense is required to be a civilian; discipline among the soldiers enables them to coexist peacefully with the civilian head of the department.

Furthermore, the law always obliges military members to embrace discipline at all times. In South Sudan, for instance, when there is an accusation among the officials of the army pertaining to infringement of civilians' rights, an investigation involving the officer in question is to be carried out in accordance with Section 87 of the SPLA Act 2009. If it is established that the officer is guilty, the law then prescribes the punishment as encoded in the Act. This type of provision promotes peaceful coexistence among the military members and civilians, as it regulates the conduct of military members.

Military members are required to adhere to the limits of operation so that they don't get into conflict with innocent civilians. Civilians are also expected to reciprocate this discipline to ensure harmony and responsible actions between the two groups. The members of the military are not permitted to provoke civilians through their actions, and likewise, civilians are expected not to provoke members of the military. This practice alleviates the animosity that might otherwise exist between the two categories of citizens.

Enhancing Protection of Civilians and their Property

Protection of civilians is the core mandate and sole responsibility of the military in every country. Discipline among the military members also enables them to respond to the matters of security that are affecting the civilians within or outside the country's borders. However, the civilians are also expected to cooperate with the operations of the military to ensure the efficiency of the security service. Efficient operations require maximum discipline of the military members to respond to the deployment instructions without manipulating the orders. Civilians must also be disciplined in order to cooperate with the army in their operations. Such an operation may be civilians' disarmament or any other form of activity.

In a state of emergency, for example, the members of the military are mandated to protect civilians, so civilians may be required to remain indoors to ensure that the military members do not interfere with them. Military members are obligated to respond to disasters and help with rescuing civilians and their property without committing any type of wrongdoing.

In this case, discipline is beneficial to the military and civilians alike, as it enables the military to carry out their rescue mission efficiently and with confidence. When such cooperation is in place, the military members will act with discipline for the advantage of the civilians. When there is a fire, for instance, the military officers are expected to act with discipline and take the rescue task seriously so that civilians do not suffer loss of their property to the fire. In the same way, civilians are also expected to pay their taxes regularly to make sure that the operations of the military officers don't have to stop due to lack of funds.

Increasing Recognition Among the Military and the Civilians

In the army, recognition of titles is an essential aspect of their philosophy. The discipline within the military settings always compels recognition of titles. Junior members of the army are obliged by the code of conduct to show respect to their seniors and address them with their titles. The same applies to civilians, whose sense of discipline for the military members leads them to address them with their titles.

Discipline also enables the civilians to acknowledge the army officers even after they have retired from active military service. Such a show of honor and recognition of army officers' occupations promotes cordial relations between the military and the civil population.

Such discipline allows for the flexibility among the military members to remain far from their families when they are deployed. The families of the military members must also have the discipline to refrain from living in the combat zones or other risky areas. Their loved ones, such as their spouses and children, must also accept such restrictions without complaint.

The discipline among the military members to wear their uniforms enables the civilians to acknowledge them as the national army, which avoids confusion between civilians and military members. Even within the army, soldiers are not allowed to undertake military operations without wearing a uniform because the other soldiers might mistake them for the enemy.

Uniformity of the troops in wartime promotes the efficiency of the forces. Staying in uniform during the war also fosters cooperation among the members of the military, whose sole objective is to defeat the common enemy. Being in uniform is mandatory, and this self-discipline helps members of the military to identify each other with ease.

Additionally, the fact that civilians do not wear military uniforms is a show of respect and recognition of the army. It means that the army uniform is only intended for those serving in the military.

Heightening Competency

In the army, discipline is seen as a means of promoting efficacy before, during, and after the military operations. Discipline enables soldiers to adhere to the rules that guide the military operations, and it enhances their efficiency during times of war. It also compels the troops to follow the orders of their senior officers while participating in war.

Moreover, discipline among military members and civilians enhances the management of the country's security and its ability to protect the civilian population and their property. As such, civilians are required to render maximum respect and cooperation to the soldiers in the process of military operations to improve the efficiency of their mission. Such cooperation may be in the form of information-sharing on security matters and other issues considered as threats to the nation.

This discipline also allows for the efficient protection of the civilians' businesses. Disciplined soldiers are responsible for defending the country and the property of the civil population within the country's boundaries. All civilians benefit from the nature of protection provided by the military members without distinction.

Promoting Integrity Among the Civilians and the Military

Discipline enables the soldiers to act with integrity in their military operations. Military members are not allowed to use their weapons to harm civilians. With this, civilians benefit from the discipline that demands the military members not to use such weapons to attack innocent civilians. On the other hand, the integrity of the civilians is enhanced through the discipline they accord to the military members.

Another aspect of integrity is that civilians have a responsibility to ensure that they provide accurate information to the military officers in the process of an investigation. Discipline strengthens integrity among the military members and the civilians, and this discipline is of paramount importance not only for their coexistence but also for the peace, security, and stability of any country.

In sum, discipline among civilians and the military contributes to the improvement of military competency, protection of the civilians, promotion of national integration, and recognition among the civilians and military members. As such, the sense of discipline is of great significance among the civilians and the military members for efficiency in security and other operations in the country.

FIFTEEN

PEACEMAKING

"A world committed to peace, a world in which we are all a family, a world in which we are all heard, cared for and loved."
Archbishop Desmond Tutu

IN CHAPTER FOURTEEN, we discussed discipline, its significance, and where to apply it. In this chapter, we are going to talk about peacemaking and understand why it is important for us as good citizens to promote peace in our society. As part of peacemaking, we will also examine a number of case studies from other countries in order to inform our understanding about peacemaking, peacebuilding, and peacekeeping. The peace of your country is in your hands as a good citizen. You have a responsibility to resolve local conflict, promote reconciliation, protect women's rights, and advocate for the inclusion of vulnerable groups and women in decision-making processes.

In the age of protracted and devastating civil wars in many parts of the world, particularly in Africa and Asia, the demand for peace and stability has increased. Fortunately, many regional and international organizations seem to be showing interest in supporting world peace than ever before. For about seven decades, civil wars have come in different dimensions and colorations, with some being viewed as political conflicts, while others are seen as religious and communal conflicts. The prevalence of peace is paramount in any country, as no meaningful economic development can take place without it. Given the choice between war and peace, I hope we can all agree that even the worst peace is better than the best war, because the best war is still destructive, while the worst peace saves lives.

Although the term is always being uttered by people on a daily basis, just like they frequently use the word love, joy, truth, or beauty, it is paradoxical that when one is asked to define peace, it becomes very difficult to give a satisfactory meaning. The Oxford Advanced Learner's Dictionary defines it as "a state of freedom from war." However, Albert Einstein would view this as tacky and intellectually weak, as he considered peace to be not only the absence of war but also the presence of justice.

Taking a look at Africa, the continent has been viewed as a den of armed conflict and instability since the 1960s. For over seven decades, the most violent and devastating conflicts have notably been intra-state, with considerable peacekeeping consequences for regional and international role-players. These conflicts have led to the internal displacement of civilians, refugees, despair, destitution, poverty, and endemic disease. Sad to say, such armed conflicts on the African continent have seriously undermined the attainment of development, security, and democratic consolidation for a very long time, despite the international push for transformation and change.

Without a sense of stability, it is likely that there will be little chance for economic development, reform, and growth. In the twenty-first century, regional countries have begun to be actively involved in peacekeeping processes to resolve intra-state conflicts and to build a foundation for the durable peace necessary for economic development. Such responsibility has abridged the traditional role played by the international community in the past.

Over the past decades, the field of peace studies has birthed a number of competing approaches to address conflict in any setting, including conflict prevention, conflict management, conflict resolution, conflict transformation, peacebuilding, and peacekeeping.

Because of these conflicting approaches to the actions or policies it encompasses, conflict prevention is arguably an ambiguous concept. However, progress toward what the Institute for Economics and Peace calls "Positive Peace" can still be identified and measured.

A 2017 report published by the Institute for Economics and Peace establishes that conflict had prevented many countries from reaching their development goals, as losses from conflict in 2015 alone were estimated at nearly US$742 billion. The report argues that by understanding the economic shocks caused by violence, "governments and policymakers can better understand how a lack of peace affecting not only economic growth but also poverty levels, social mobility, education, the control of corruption or life expectancy" (8). As citizens of this beautiful nation, we should also expect our good government officials from the executive, judiciary, and legislature to take note of this as they run the country.

Peacebuilding

The term "peacebuilding" was coined in 1975 by the renowned Norwegian sociologist Johan Galtung, who identified three approaches to peace: peacekeeping, peacemaking, and peacebuilding. He argued that peacebuilding "has a structure different from, perhaps over and above, peacekeeping and ad hoc peacemaking." Galtung believes that peace structures should be created that produce alternatives to war and eliminate the potential causes of it.

Although the term has no standard definition, one commonly quoted description of peacebuilding is that it is "a process that facilitates the establishment of durable peace and tries to prevent the recurrence of violence by addressing root causes and effects of conflict through reconciliation, institution building, and political as well as economic transformation."

In 2007, the UN Secretary-General's Policy Committee defined peacebuilding as "a range of measures targeted to reduce the risk of lapsing or relapsing into conflict by strengthening national capacities at all levels for conflict management and to lay the foundations for sustainable peace and development." When it is understood this way, the next step would be to scrutinize the critical ways in which donors and governments can tackle the sources of violence and address the weak institutional and state capacities that contribute to internal conflict and violence.

After the end of World War II in 1945, the United States and its allies established international initiatives such as the Bretton Woods institutions and the Marshall Plan aimed at rebuilding Europe following the devastation caused by the war. These initiatives were conceived in terms of peacekeeping and peacemaking, although they would have been termed as peacebuilding activities if the term had existed then.

In post-conflict regions, peacebuilding activities are always geared at addressing the underlying causes of the conflict. For instance, in post-Cold War Bosnia and Herzegovina, the international community intervened to rebuild the nation. This global effort was exemplary in fostering self-sustaining peace in the aftermath of a deadly drawn-out internal conflict that claimed tens of thousands of civilians' lives. Although there were other such operations in places including Kosovo, Macedonia, and Afghanistan, the one in Bosnia and Herzegovina was one of the first, and still among the interventions with the most financial support.

It is believed that democratization and legitimate and accountable governance can prevent the recurrence of new cycles of violence. In some countries, peacebuilding activities are combined and implemented alongside state-building activities. For instance, when South Sudan achieved peace and the Revitalized Transitional Government of National Unity (R-TGoNU) was formed in 2020, a Ministry of Peacebuilding was also created. This new ministry was mandated by the peace agreement to spearhead the reconciliation process across the country, especially among the communities whose social fabric was weakened by the seven-year-old civil war.

Peacekeeping

The term "peacekeeping" is defined as an act of preserving peace specifically between hostile groups or states, especially by a sanctioned military force. Peacekeeping encompasses several activities aimed at creating the conditions for lasting peace. According to the UN, peacekeepers can include soldiers, police officers, and civilian personnel. Since its inception, peacekeeping has contributed to a reduction in wartime deaths, both on the battlefield and among civilians, and in the risk of renewed warfare in most countries formerly engaged in active civil war.

For decades, there has been a general understanding among UN nation-state governments and organizations that peacekeepers have a mandate to monitor and observe peace processes in post-conflict settings and to assist former combatants in implementing commitments established in peace agreements. Such assistance can come in many forms, such as support for free and fair elections, power-sharing arrangements, and economic and social development.

In addition to the United Nations, there are other organizations that work to promote world peace and implement peacekeeping work. Examples of non-UN peacekeeping organizations include the UN-authorized NATO mission in Kosovo, the Multinational Force and Observers on the Sinai Peninsula, and efforts organized by the European Union and the African Union. In addition to the UN, there is the Nonviolent Peaceforce, which is known for its expertise in general peacemaking.

Because they take a neutral stance in the conflicts in the regions where they are deployed, peacekeepers are considered non-combatants. This exposes them to attacks, insecurity of their property, and aggression of belligerents in most host states. Since the late 1990s, peacekeepers have been seen as vanguards in the protection of civilians in countries ravaged by armed conflict.

When South Sudan lapsed into civil war in the year 2013, many civilians who were uprooted from their homes by the armed conflict fled into the United Nations Protection of Civilians Sites, although some crossed the international borders to seek further refuge. Over 200,000 Internally Displaced Persons were hosted by the United Nations Mission in South Sudan (UNMISS) in its Protection of Civilians sites across the country.

Until January 2016, UNMISS Bentiu's Protection of Civilians Site alone was hosting about 143,000 IDPs, making it the largest IDP camp in the whole country. However, many civilians who did not make it to the IDP camps fled to the swamps and bushes for hiding. This category of civilians were the ones who bore the brunt of war, as they were feeding on waterlily and wild fruits for survival, with some going for days without food in the jungle of South Sudan.

Women's Participation in Peace Processes

Women's role in peacekeeping and peacemaking has always been underestimated. Mediation processes and all aspects of peace processes have been considered man's responsibility, as women's place is seen to be in the kitchen. However, in the year 2000, the United Nations Security Council passed Resolution 1325, spurring a widespread local and global policy engagement in developing programs and networks designed to implement it. The resolution was aimed at including women in the peace processes as active and equal actors in the prevention and resolution of conflicts, peace negotiations, peace-building, peacekeeping, humanitarian response, and post-conflict reconstruction. The resolution stressed the importance of their equal participation and full involvement in all efforts for the maintenance and promotion of peace and security around the world.

In 2010, exactly ten years after the adoption of the resolution, researchers studied the impact of Resolution 1325 to assess its success. However, they found that there was limited success with the imple-mentation, particularly in the clause about the increase in women's participation in peace negotiations and peace agreements. Moreover, sexual and gender-based violence continued to be prevalent, despite efforts to mitigate it.

This worrisome scenario forced the same Security Council to pass Resolution 2122 unanimously in 2013. This new resolution calls for stronger measures regarding women's participation in conflict and post-conflict processes such as peace talks, gender expertise in peace-keeping missions, improved information about the impact of armed conflict on women, and more direct briefing to the Council on progress in these areas.

In the same year, UN's Committee on the Elimination of Discrimination against Women (CEDAW) said in a general recommendation that any state that has ratified the UN Women's Rights Convention would be obliged to uphold women's rights before, during, and after conflict. This obligation includes but is not limited to states that are directly involved in fighting or those that provide troops or donor assistance for conflict prevention, humanitarian aid, or post-conflict reconstruction. Concerning accountability and access to justice, they also stated that ratifying states should exercise due diligence in ensuring that non-state actors, such as armed groups and private security contractors, be held accountable for crimes against women. As good citizens, we have a responsibility to abide by international and national laws that protect women's rights and accord them a space in decision-making processes at all levels.

Effects of Gender-Based Violence on Women

Even though gender encompasses both men and women, the main focus remains on women, as they have traditionally been excluded or subsumed under "men," especially during armed conflict. Sexual violence and other forms of gender-based violence are higher in areas of armed conflict than in non-conflict-affected settings. The vast majority of people who have suffered gender-based violence are women and girls.

The reason why we are required to protect women against the menace of gender-based violence (GBV) is because when they are subjected to such abuse, it destroys them physically, psychologically, socially, and economically. To be specific, psychological trauma, physical injuries, stigmatization, and inability to participate in economic activities are some of the major effects of gender-based violence. GBV can deprive women of confidence, constrain their movement, and hamper their ability to reach their full potential in life.

Whenever gender-based violence is mentioned, what readily comes into our minds is violence perpetrated against women and girls. Although men are also known to suffer from GBV, the magnitude is near insignificant as compared to that of women because of patriarchal values that accord women a lower social status in the society. In some settings, women see it as a joke or unrealistic when we talk of the impact of gender-based violence on men, since they feel that men are only the perpetrators of the crime.

When we talk about the impacts, the first thing that comes into our mind is physical harm, because this is what we can see when we are assessing the condition of a physically abused woman. Such physical effects include injury of the victim, disability in the reproductive organs, and chronic health problems such as irritable bowel syndrome, gastrointestinal disorders, various chronic syndromes, hypertension, and others. Sexual and reproductive health problems resulting from contracting sexually transmitted diseases such as HIV/AIDS, or from high-risk pregnancies, also cause long-term if not permanent stigma.

Another serious effect of gender-based violence, as mentioned above, is psychological trauma, which includes both direct and indirect phenomena. While direct psychological effects might be paralysis, mental disorder, anxiety, fear, mistrust of others, inability to concentrate, loneliness, depression, suicide, post-traumatic stress, emotional pain, or a sense of denial, the indirect stigma comprises psychosomatic illnesses, alcohol or drug use, and withdrawal. Victims of psychological trauma sometimes experience nightmares or are haunted by fear and feelings of shame or guilt.

The third factor is social impact, which is also very painful and costly to survivors of this menace. Some of the effects include rejection by family members or by society, stigmatization, further sexual exploitation, and severe punishment. In most cases, the social impact of gender-based violence affects the development and wellbeing of children and families in the society. For instance, boys who witness brutality against their mothers are likely to be of a violent disposition, while girls grow into fearful victims. When school-aged girls are subjected to gender-based violence, they tend to avoid school due to shame. Such avoidance may result in poor performance at school, thus depriving the society of full participation of women in developmental activities.

Acute fear of future violence, which extends beyond the individual survivors to other members of the community, is the most worrying implication of gender-based violence in this category. When victims feel a sense of rejection, isolation, ostracism, and social stigma at the community level, they resort to the consumption of alcohol and other dangerous drugs in an attempt to relieve the stress. However, excessive use of these drugs always leads to addiction rather than the intended objective of stress management.

The fourth effect is enormous financial consequences on the victims, as it reduces their ability to participate in economic activities in society. Most households affected by GBV face economic hardship in the form of increased expenses and/or loss of income or productivity due to the health impacts of violence on women, as fear of venturing into public spaces damages women's confidence. Such fear can often curtail women's education, which can in turn limit their income-generating opportunities. Absenteeism from the workplace because of violence inflicted on them by their spouses and other perpetrators can cost women their jobs too. This increases women's vulnerability, as it negatively impacts their income-generating power.

Financial hardship caused by violence against women could lead to household dissolution or even homelessness, especially when there is no familial or formal social support for affected women and their families. Sometimes, survivors cannot count on familial support due to the stigma attached to experiencing GBV. In the absence of familial and public support for survivors, families are burdened by hospital bills when survivors require medical care for physical injuries, pregnancy, sexually transmitted diseases, or mental health issues triggered by GBV and sexual violence. In a situation where a woman is no longer able to care for her children due to long-term injury, death, or other circumstances, the need to care for her children becomes an additional financial burden to the surviving relatives.

For many centuries, perhaps since the creation of the universe, women have suffered from man's brutality, which often comes in the form of physical and sexual violence. With the rise of feminist movements around the world, including within the UN system over the last century, a consensus was reached at the United Nations Security Council meeting to open a space for women after it was realized that their plight is real and requires global attention. This led to the passing of UNSC Resolution 1325 in the year 2000, as indicated earlier in this chapter. The resolution empowers women to participate in peace processes, with the aim of presenting women's issues such as GBV and wartime sexual-related violence.

In solidarity with women, the former President of Liberia and Nobel Laureate H.E. Ellen Johnson Sirleaf once said that women have become the greatest victims of war and the biggest stakeholders of peace, affirming her earlier stance as a women's activist — a role she played in her country during the liberation struggle. Such a sentiment is shared by many peacemakers, as it is believed that most peace agreements negotiated with the involvement of women always witness a greater breakthrough than the ones purely dominated by men.

Good citizens treat people with fairness, as they don't discriminate against anyone. If you are created as a man, you don't have a right to discriminate against a woman, because you didn't choose that gender. Whenever you are tempted to be brutal with a woman, ask yourself the question: "If I were a woman, would I deserve this brutality?"

Protection of Vulnerable Groups During Wartime

The phrase "vulnerable group during wartime" encompasses women, children, elderly, sick, wounded, and those with disabilities. These groups require special protection from the warring parties and external actors during wartime, as they always bear the utmost brunt of the conflict compared to other groups in the society. As vulnerable as they are, they can hardly protect themselves from the fighters. In many instances, women are sexually abused by fighters who use sex as a weapon of war during the armed conflict. Children, on the other hand, are conscripted by the warring parties to join the fight. Old citizens, sick, wounded, and people with disabilities who cannot escape risk facing the wrath of undisciplined fighters who either lack humanity or could not distinguish between a combatant and non-combatant.

In intra-state wars, fighters are required to be guided by rules of engagement to avoid targeting civilians and non-combatants. This involves applying the protocols enshrined in the Geneva Convention pertaining to rules of engagement. According to Dr. Regeena Kingsley (2017), "the imposition of restrictive rules on armed forces during wartime is not a new practice." Evidence of their use, according to her, is found as early as the royal "Letters of Marque and Reprisal" commissions issued to fourteenth-century knights, as well as "within similar commissions and charters given to privateers plundering foreign trade ships in the Elizabethan era of the sixteenth century."

Our modern understanding of rules of engagement arose in reaction to the violence of World War I, with French Prime Minister Georges Clemenceau famously saying that "war is much too serious a matter to be left to military men." Governments reached a consensus that the use and degree of force employed by armed forces should no longer "be decided solely by the commanders," but by an internationally binding framework.

While rules of engagement are important, the protection of women from rapists is equally important, and it requires the utmost attention of the army commanders and political leaders during wartime. In any country, rape crime and other forms of violence against women are complex and require holistic solutions with the concerted intervention of a wide variety of actors ranging from government, civil society, faith-based groups, UN agencies, and NGOs to bilateral and multilateral funding institutions. A high degree of coordination across sectors and areas of intervention from all levels is always critical in achieving the aforementioned aspiration.

There is also a need for strong partnerships, particularly among institutions with shared vision and determination, to help the government and other actors to establish coherent policies that enhance human rights. In order to remove obstacles obstructing women's rights and freedom and help them fight their cause more effectively, they also need to be empowered and equipped with all necessary tools to combat all forms of human rights violations and gender abuse. This includes the provision of training skills on access to justice and the prevention of sexual violence, among others.

Fundamental reform in the area of the justice system is crucially important in order to address the needs of victims and survivors of GBV, including those who experienced violence during violent conflict. In post-conflict situations, women sometimes seem to be less represented in various institutions, including the police and army, as well as in the private sector. This needs to be corrected, and for this reason, there is a need to introduce special police units with a preponderance of female police officers, with a mandate to deal mainly with GBV issues. This unit should also be equipped with psychosocial support counselors and healthcare workers trained in women's reproductive health, HIV/AIDS counseling, and other lethal sexually transmitted diseases (STDs).

GBV victims should also be helped to cope with distressing experiences and wartime memories that have had a negative impact on their lives. In many post-conflict settings, institutions are established to help them see the need for non-judgmental, compassionate, non-rejecting approaches, including the care for survivors or victims of violence. Moreover, they are made to understand their beliefs more fully in light of human rights laws, religion, culture, and tradition.

Women's vulnerability as victims of gender-based violence has become an essential focus of any comprehensive conflict analysis or strategy for peacebuilding. For instance, the particular concerns of women such as protection, reproductive health care, capacity building, financial empowerment, political participation, and access to land have also become commonplace claims since the last quarter of the twentieth century.

Additionally, many studies address the particular situation of women and children both in times of war and in times of peace. Most policy reports about gender in armed conflict found that women and children are always portrayed as the victims of male violence. Oftentimes, when attention is paid to men as victims, it is assumed that the perpetrators are also male, despite the fact that both men and women can be either victims or perpetrators.

National Healing and Reconciliation

Healing is understood as any strategy, process, or activity that improves the psychological health of individuals following extensive violent conflict, while reconciliation, is the reestablishment of friendly relations after the conflict. Both processes are very important whenever conflict dwindles down. After South Sudan gained her independence from Sudan in the year 2011, there was no meaningful agenda for reconciliation among the South Sudanese to heal the wounds left open by internal fighting during the twenty-one years of civil war.

Most of these internal conflicts were fomented by ideological differences and ethnic rivalries during the war. It is believed that if the government had reconciled the communities in the immediate aftermath of the separation, the country wouldn't have witnessed the deadly civil war which obliterated the prospects for unity and peaceful coexistence among the people of South Sudan in 2013. And if it had happened, the magnitude wouldn't have reached the extent that it did. For a reconciliation to be successful, one needs a comprehensive environmental understanding to employ the appropriate methods in a reconciliation process effectively.

While international support in this regard is always welcome, a homegrown process is usually seen to produce the most effective outcome. This is because outsiders sometimes do not fully understand a complex social system in a society as well as those who are part of that system.

In most reconciliation processes, security is always considered a general prerequisite, since it helps in the restoration of trust and confidence among the citizens, as a lack of confidence and trust among the civil population serves as a major obstacle to any reconciliation process. Security, in any setting, "begins with the cessation of hostilities through a cease-fire agreement or separation of the conflicting groups by the establishment of a demilitarized zone" (Buckeye 2010, 16).

However, such fears can only diminish if the security arrangement results in a meaningful military integration, amalgamation, or impartial law enforcement that the public can trust. Some societies may not be able to progress in any other dimension until justice is fully served. Structurally, justice requires the implementation or revision of a constitution and legal system that abolishes discrimination and guarantees all individuals equal protection under the law. "The establishment of an impartial judiciary is not only essential but exceptionally difficult in a divided and polarized society" (Buckeye 2010, 16). US Army Major Terrence H. Buckeye further explains:

> Also critical is the restructuring of government to a representative system with an eventual goal of democracy. While many reconciliation experts believe that democracy is a first step or pre-condition in the reconciliation process, aggrieved parties in a divided society who feel that justice and truth have not been adequately addressed may simply resume their power struggle through the ballot box. Without adequate progress in reconciliation, the losing party may not be able to accept political defeat and return to armed conflict. Economically, the structure of the new state must ensure equitable economic development and opportunity as

well as provide reparations or restitution to people who had property confiscated or destroyed unjustly during the conflict.

[...] The psychological aspects of justice are even more difficult and contextually sensitive than structural aspects. Whether to engage in a process of retributive justice, amnesty, restorative justice, or a multi-faceted approach depends entirely on the sensitivities of the situation's context. Retributive justice seeks to punish perpetrators of crimes. Advocates of retributive justice say that retributive justice avoids unbridled revenge [...] fulfills an obligation to the victims, individualizes guilt, strengthens legitimacy and the process of democratization, and breaks the cycle of impunity. Critics of retributive justice contend that it may be unfeasible due to political circumstances, risks destabilizing a fragile peace [...] ignores the feelings and needs of victims, may have crippling effects on governance, and may thwart the reconciliation process if done with an impartial judiciary. (16-17)

For a lasting peace to prevail in any country, justice is always the only way to go. Local justice structures are vital in providing justice, since they know the context better than external tribunals. This worked in post-war Rwanda with the introduction of Gacaca courts.

After the deadly genocide that claimed about a million lives, the Rwandan government established around 12,000 community-based courts known as Gacaca across the country to try genocide criminals as well as to promote forgiveness by victims, ownership of guilt by criminals, and reconciliation among the communities as a way of facilitating communal healing and rebuilding. Approximately 115,000 defendants accused of atrocities during the country's genocide were shifted into that traditional justice system for trial.

The traditional justice method was placed in the hands of trusted citizens such as religious leaders, village elders, and local officials in resolving domestic or communal conflicts, including rape and domestic violence during the war. This local justice system, which operated from 2005 until the end of its mandate in mid-July 2010, was a big boost to justice as it supported the national courts and ad hoc international tribunal court based in Arusha in dealing with category four cases, which may take decades to try by the international court that only tackles category one crimes.

In a situation where national tribunals are impractical due to the absence of an impartial judiciary, the hybrid courts and international tribunals such as the International Criminal Court sometimes provide an alternative. A case in point is that of the former Yugoslavia, where the United Nations, in the aftermath of the conflict, formed a court of law called the International Criminal Tribunal for the former Yugoslavia (ICTY) to try the war crimes that were committed during the conflicts in the Balkans in the 1990s.

Another method of transitional justice, which is also considered to play a positive role, is amnesty. Although it is subject to criticism by those who consider it a miscarriage of justice, amnesty may be appropriate in situations where the conflict follows the laws regulating military operations in a war that is predominantly between uniformed personnel. However, "in most intra-state conflicts where civilian atrocities occurred, amnesty is an inappropriate method for justice. As IDEA [International Institute for Democracy and Electoral Assistance] notes, 'Reconciliation processes are ineffective as long as the vicious circle of impunity is not broken'" (Buckeye 2010, 17).

Resolving Local Conflicts

National and local-level conflict schemes are both interconnected and distinct in most countries unraveled by intra-state and intercommunal conflicts. For instance, we say the two are interconnected if there is evidence that the local conflicts are caused and driven by the same factors that determine the national conflict system. On the other hand, they may stand alone, particularly if there is no political factor connecting them.

In a situation where there is a link between the two levels of conflict, it is always challenging and effort demanding to disentangle the two. Ghana provides one of the best examples of interconnect-edness between local and national conflict systems. In the year 2002, a violent conflict broke out in Ghana's Dagomba Kingdom on the issue of succession to the throne. This conflict threatened Ghana's national security because the two main national political parties got involved, supporting opposing sides.

At the time, the country was approaching an election, which was to be held in 2004. Ghana has a history of violent inter-community conflicts, particularly in the northern part of the country. For instance, between 1990 and 2002, there were fourteen violent clashes between two tribes of Northern Ghana. In 1994 and 1995, there was a violent clash between the Konkomba and Nanumba ethnic groups in which 5000 people were killed.

Sometimes, it is of paramount importance to deal with different levels of conflict separately rather than assuming that the two are intertwined and viewing the local conflict as an extension of the national system. In most instances, achieving a national peace is enough to bring peace at a local level. However, this may not be the case in other situations where structural causes of conflict are difficult to resolve either because of the involvement of politicians, as seen above in the case of Ghana, or due to natural circumstances such as discovery of a mineral resource at the borderline of two neighboring communities.

Most local conflicts start as stand-alone and later result in a vicious cycle because of politicians' and army commanders' interference. For instance, a fight may erupt between two clans as a normal conflict. However, when casualties are massive, army commanders and government officials with influence in the community may show their solidarity by supplying arms to the parties to the conflict such that they go for revenge and prolong the fighting. This is the same with cattle raiding and conflicts that spring from land dispute.

Managing these conflicts sometimes requires political will and strict measures against the spoilers. The first step is comprehensive civilian disarmament. When the situation stabilizes, the actors, which in this case are termed as spoilers, need to be identified and to undergo disciplinary actions.

Communal conflict in most countries has an appalling effect on the economies and stability of nations. Communities that experience conflict always live in fear due to insecurity, displacement, and killing. In a situation where there is displacement, poverty always engulfs the community as people are denied a chance at productivity. When governments want to manage the conflict, it is wise to take a peaceful approach. Sending security forces to stabilize the situation may only add fuel to the conflict instead of resolving it. After a conflict subsides, it is wise to send local peacebuilders to defuse the conflict. These were used in Ghana, and today it has boosted the country's image as one of Africa's most stable democracies.

Kenya is also another example where a local peace committee used a bottom-up process to establish a peace architecture in a country ravaged by communal conflict. In 1993, a group of women from the Wajir district, which borders Somalia and Ethiopia, initiated a peace process in order to resolve a deadly inter-clan conflict. At the time, there was a highly destructive cycle of violent conflict between different clans of Kenyan Somalis, leading to more than 1200 deaths over a period of four years.

This conflict was caused by a number of factors including a weak district government that was unable to regulate conflict; lack of development; a physical environment prone to droughts, which produced scarce natural resources to sustain the population; a pastoralist culture that condoned livestock raiding; an influx of refugees from Somalia and Ethiopia; and proliferation of small arms. The civil society group of predominantly women embarked on the peace sensitization process in the area to promote peaceful coexistence among the clans. They started by engaging the elders of different clans in a mediation process. After several meetings, the elders agreed to sign a code of conduct referred to as the Al Fatah Declaration.

During this process, the local peace committee, on a voluntary basis, worked with and involved representatives of formal authority, particularly the district commissioner and the Member of Parliament. In 2001, the process that started as a local peace committee turned into a national institution known as the National Steering Committee on Peacebuilding and Conflict Management, with an aim of formulating a national policy on conflict management and coordinating various peacebuilding initiatives, including the local peace committees.

Managing local conflict is often a difficult task, especially when there is an active intra-state conflict. When South Sudan lapsed into civil war in 2013, citizens were polarized, including the military, politicians, and civilians alike. The war affected many states across the country. However, one of the states that was most heavily affected in the early months of the conflict was Unity State, where the community was divided along political lines, with some supporting the government and others supporting the opposition. The division was extreme, as civilians with opposing political views did not want to look each other in the eye, let alone talk or eat together.

Within the state, there was a United Nations Protection of Civilians site (POC), inhabited by over 140,000 Internally Displaced Persons. These people were more sympathetic to the opposition than to the government. To them, whoever lives outside the camp, particularly in Bentiu town, was considered a government supporter. At the same time, those living in the town of Bentiu perceived those living inside the IDP camp as pro-opposition. The two groups were stereotyping each other, thus making it difficult for the local peace actors to bring them together at the reconciliation table.

In 2014, the United Nations Mission in South Sudan's Department of Civil Affairs in Bentiu Field Office, where this author served as Civil Affairs Officer at the time, took the initiative to try the reconciliation process. Religious leaders representing the two groups were invited to hold their first meeting inside the UN premises. However, this first meeting did not take place because the religious leaders inside the POC were threatened by the IDPs, including the camp leadership, for initiating a dialogue with enemies. The meeting was canceled indefinitely, thus burying the hope for peace dialogue. The UN staff did not give up, and fresh consultations were made with different community structures, including the IDP leadership. When they were convinced and allowed the religious leaders to go ahead with the meeting, Civil Affairs Officers set a new date for the religious leaders to meet.

The meeting took place on the same UN premises, as agreed earlier. During the meeting, a host of issues including security, peace, and reconciliation were discussed. The two sides cited hatred and extremism as dividing factors. As such, they resolved to spearhead the reconciliation process in their respective denominations and communities. One of the resolutions was to meet with the military commanders from both sides to discuss the prevailing insecurity and protection of women from rape. This first meeting opened a door for other community structures such as women, youth, and traditional chiefs from both political divides to also conduct meetings, which later turned into a monthly meeting.

When enough trust was gained a few months later, there was also flexibility in the choice of the venue, as they could meet either in town or at the POC site. After regular engagement and a series of communal meetings, the rate of animosities and stereotypes scaled down drastically. The insecurity, which used to be rampant, especially in the vicinity of the POC site, improved unexpectedly. There was also a reduction in rape cases among the women who used to go and collect firewood in the bush. More importantly, there was free movement of civilians between the UNMISS protection of the Civilians site and Bentiu town.

Stopping conflict and promoting peaceful coexistence and social cohesion is very important for the development and progress of any country. However, it takes a good citizen with humanity at heart to make it a success.

In a ministerial communiqué of the Organization for Economic Co-operation and Development (OECD) made in 2001, the thirty member states regarded social cohesion as "a central objective of sustainable development" that has to be embraced. The OECD countries made ongoing commitments to fight social exclusion by enhancing access to employment and learning opportunities.

The education ministers in the same communiqué also acknowledged the importance of equitable access to learning opportunities as a major policy concern. They underscored that "sustainable development and social cohesion depend critically on the competencies of all of our population." The OECD aims to address these issues across the spectrum of its work, valuing both efficiency and equity. For the last sixty years, most international and regional organizations have come to the realization that education is one of the most important tools that a good citizen can use to solve societal problems and transform lives.

SIXTEEN

RESPONSIBILITY

"The moment you take responsibility for everything in your life
is the moment you can change anything in your life."
Hal Elrod

In chapter fifteen, we discussed peacemaking and understood why it is important for good citizens to promote peace in the society. In this last chapter, we are going to focus on responsibility and its different types.

Responsibility is the skill of becoming accountable and responding to a situation in a wise manner. Responsible citizenship is a vital factor in developing a country's national identity and civic awareness that can lead to political, social, and economic stability. These three factors, if adhered to, can enable every one of us to reap the fruits of collective success we all labored for. Citizens are expected to act responsibly by doing their duty to ensure that standards and the quality of services and products are both moral and ethical, and that they constitute an effective "return on investment" to the ordinary consumer, both domestically and internationally.

In the year 2000, world leaders held one of their remarkable summits where they produced Millennium Development Goals, including eight objectives. These goals cover social as well as environmental issues, primary education for all, eradicating extreme poverty and hunger, and health. In that summit, global warming was blamed for most of the health problems. As a result, participants spelled out some principles regulating global warming. Leaders were obliged to ratify and adopt the resolutions of the summit upon their return to their respective countries.

Today, citizens in every country are still expected to adhere to the summit's outcomes, particularly the need to make the world clean and a better place for living. As citizens, we need to continue our efforts to reduce the negative impact of climate change, which is having such a profound effect on the economy and our health.

It is said that if you cannot explain it to a six-year-old child, then you do not have mastery of the subject. A primary school child who is reading this may find it difficult to understand what the writer means about global warming or climate change. Environmentalists have divided sources of pollution into two major categories: natural and anthropogenic sources. Natural sources are those that emanate from the natural environment that releases pollutants, which contaminate the environment. Examples of these sources are mainly natural calamities such as volcanic eruptions and forest fires, which release large amounts of carbon dioxide and other harmful gases and material into the environment.

The second source of pollution is anthropogenic sources, also referred to as man-made sources. As the name illustrates, these are man-made sources or activities caused by humans that release pollutants and toxins that harm the environment. Some common examples of human-made sources of pollution include the burning of fossil fuels for energy generation, emissions from various modes of transportation, agricultural waste runoff, oil spills, and improper waste management and disposal. In a less industrialized country like South Sudan, the most common sources of environmental pollution are oil spills and poor waste management.

Sometime when you drink a soda in a plastic bottle, you may throw the empty bottle on the street. In the back of your mind, you think that it is only one bottle and it has no effect. While doing this, you have to be reminded that there is another citizen who is doing the same thing, with the same mindset of seeing that bottle as just a single bottle that has no effect.

Let's assume that the entire population of South Sudan of more than twelve million each buys at least one plastic bottle of soda daily. After drinking it, everybody throws his or her bottle in an open area, since we all share the same mindset that it is just a single bottle. How many bottles do you think we can dispose of in an open area in a single day? A simple calculation shows that we would dump more than twelve million plastic bottles on our streets in only a single day. Let's assume that we repeat the same practice on the following day, or for a whole month or a year. I believe we would have a country but only a gigantic garbage pile of plastic bottles.

In today's world, a citizen's responsibility also goes beyond his or her own country's borders. Tourism, for instance, affects not just a country's economy, but also its culture and traditions. The modern trend toward sustainable tourism emphasizes that the visitors to a country, not only the hosts, have certain responsibilities to preserve the destination and its local culture. You may be that tourist in another country. When it happens, you will be obliged to adhere to the environmental preservation laws of that country. Failure to comply with such principles may result in punitive measures against you. In this way, you may not only be arrested but also bring shame to the country you represent during your vacation. As a citizen, you need to take responsibility for action, your learning, and social wellbeing, and recognize your duty to represent your country positively wherever you go.

Types of Responsibility

Writer Elizabeth Wagele (2015) defines responsibility as "feeling it's your duty to deal with what comes up, being accountable, and/or being able to act independently and make decisions without authorization.

[...] Responsibility is having common sense, authority, leadership, and maturity; being reliable, trustworthy, dependable, and answerable." However, she notes that "we don't all express our ability to be responsible in the same way." In the world of responsibilities, there are different ways to express that, depending on who you are, what you know, and how it is done.

Wagele uses the nine Enneagram personality types to show how different people may express responsibility in different ways. You may be a perfectionist or a helper who feels a strong sense of responsibility for your own behavior or that of the people around you; an achiever who feels "responsible for getting ahead in the world and for leading others to get things done"; a romantic who feels responsible to himself "for honoring and expressing feelings and values and for finding beauty in life"; an adventurer with a sense of responsibility for protecting the environment around you; an asserter who feels "responsible for enforcing rules and for standing up for truth and justice"; a questioner who is aware of life's dangers and tries to avoid mistakes; or a peace seeker whose responsibility is to promote harmony and fairness in the society.

You need to get this thing right when you want to travel this path of responsibility. There is more to being responsible than just doing what other people want you to do; being responsible means making the right choices. As a responsible person, you are expected to adhere to six essential elements of honesty: compassion, respect, fairness, accountability, and courage. There are many types of responsibilities, but I will focus on only a few that I consider important as far as this book is concerned: personal agency, accountability, commitment, moral responsibilities, and social responsibilities.

Personal Agency

This type of responsibility refers to one's ability to influence things that happen to them. Individuals with a strong sense of agency take responsibility for both their successes and failures without blaming external factors such as systems, circumstances, bad luck, or other people. This sense of agency is indispensable, particularly for those who yearn to take full control of their life. "Studies have found that the healthiest people strive to increase their sense of personal power by developing competence and autonomy and by decreasing their dependence on others. Increasing your sense of competence and autonomy involves, among other things, recognizing the ways in which you can influence your own life [...] and assuming responsibility for your behavior without needing to blame others" (Lamia 2010).

The English philosopher James Allen said in his book *As Man Thinketh*, "Man is made or unmade by himself; in the armoury of thought he forges the weapons by which he destroys himself; he also fashions the tools with which he builds for himself heavenly mansions of joy and strength and peace." Those who lack agency do not take responsibility for themselves, and as such, they find it difficult to cope with the world. They keep blaming others for their own failures, spending most of their time criticizing and cursing others, while they deny themselves time to think and focus on finding solutions to the problems they consider to be hindering their success.

Blaming others all the time is not helpful for someone with a burning desire to succeed. We should stop blaming our partners, parents, financial situations, our upbringing, or our pets for our misfortunes. We need to desist from the blame game and start performing our roles as responsible citizens. For instance, if you are a married couple and you are physically fit, you have a responsibility to work and provide for your family. Your kids will always depend on you for their schooling, medication, food, and other basic needs. Your children may be unruly, your partner may be bad-tempered, and your co-worker may be intolerable, but if you, as an individual, handle such responsibility, you have also contributed to the nation-building by bringing up your children responsibly. Whatever circumstance you find yourself in, you always need to be calm and take a thoughtful moment to reflect on how you can react to the situation.

Blaming keeps you in victim mode, as it denies you a chance of changing your current situation. When you stop blaming others and accept that your life and whatever happens to it is your responsibility, you will automatically shift away from victimhood and instead become a victor. Now you can look the situation in the eye and decide what to do about it. Stop having too much reliance on others, take full charge of your life, recognize what happened to you, emphasize the power of positivity, and see yourself unmistakably.

Since no man is an island, other people may lend you a helping hand. When you are assisted, do not forget to say "thank you." Think about an area of your life in which you feel very successful and one in which you would like to be successful but are not. Ask yourself a question such as, "How can I apply the techniques that helped me to achieve success in the areas where I am not successful?" Do not forget that a healthy life is in itself a sign of wealth, so you should practice healthy self-focus all the time.

Taking responsibility for your life means taking responsibility for your powers of thinking, feeling, speaking, and acting, because this is the structure of all human experience. Do not forget that men create their own lives with their thoughts, feelings, words, and actions.

Another problem in this category is taking things personally. As a responsible person, you have to work and refuse to take anything personally. As humans, we tend to assume that everything is about us whenever we fall into trouble. Refuse to take any form of disagreement as a personal attack.

Remember, you do not have control over how other people respond; you only have control over how you respond to them. Sometimes the disagreement may not be about you, but about the issue at hand. Instead of making assumptions, ask questions. When you do that, you will realize that it is a very powerful and liberating practice with never-ending surprises. Remember again, the best way to discover your future, master your fate, and control your soul is to stop blaming others for your own failures. You have to understand that life's battles are always fought individually, so there is no point in losing control of yourself by blaming others.

Accountable Leadership

Another element of responsibility is that entrusted to you by your government or public as a civil servant, or by your community as a community leader, to manage or lead a community-based organization providing services to your people. In a government setting, when public officials — including the President, ministers, Members of Parliament, governors, ambassadors, directors, and mayors — are elected by citizens or appointed to office by the relevant authorities, they all have a duty to remain accountable to the ordinary citizens who work tirelessly to pay their wages, and to contribute to the development and welfare of the nation. In this respect, the interest of an ordinary citizen is expected to remain paramount throughout any decision-making process in all public offices in the land. Such is the responsibility allotted to the constitutional post holders by the supreme law of the land known as the Constitution.

In case the ordinary citizens who are stakeholders in the development process and economic growth become concerned about the development and economic situations, they have a right to ask questions and demand accountability from the government. Relevant authorities should exercise full responsibility with a certain degree of honesty and discipline and provide answers to the citizens' questions.

Being responsible means that you are accountable for any misdeed that happens as a result of your action. For instance, if public funds disappear and you are a boss in that institution, you have to agree to be investigated. If it is proven that you had a hand in the disappearance, you have to accept the responsibility and compensate the loss. This way, others who are mainly subordinates would also see this and start to change their behavior. Not only that, the community and those interested in serving the community when you step aside will also learn from this example and desist from following the path you traveled.

In chapter eleven, I reiterated the importance of accountability. I also emphasized that if you are unable to serve the public, you'd better go home and serve yourself — perhaps that is what you are capable of doing. If you are in a position of leadership, whether you are a governor, commissioner, town mayor, or any other such position, you have to be accountable to your subjects who gave you that authority to lead. Without them, you cannot climb that ladder of leadership. Simply put, you need to be there for them by exercising full responsibility as you expect them to be there for you.

Commitment

Commitment as a type of responsibility is a state or quality of being dedicated to a cause or an activity. Being a responsible person makes your life better. In life, when you do what you have promised to do, people will always see you as a responsible and reliable person. This also boosts your self-esteem and self-worth. Some people make promises and fail to fulfill them, which is always disastrous, as people lose trust in them.

In view of this, it is important that when you make a promise to a person, you have to be ready to take on the responsibility of keeping the promise and living up to your word. If you are not ready to respect your promise, do not make it. A promise may be verbal (informal) or in the form of a legal agreement called a contract. When you make a verbal commitment, you may be safe, but when you commit yourself to a contract and fail to respect it, you may find yourself in court.

You should understand that when you make a promise, you consent or agree to take responsibility or obligation. For instance, you may borrow $100 from a friend or take out a loan from a company. It is up to you, not your partner, friend, or family member, to refund it. You are responsible for paying it back on time, according to the length of time you both agreed on.

Moral Responsibility

Moral responsibilities are based on the principles of right and wrong. It is the simplest yet the most difficult thing to attain. It is summarized by the religious saying, "Do unto others as you would have them do unto you." People consider it tricky because it can be interpreted in many different ways. Some think of it as obeying the traditional norms of the places in which they live. Some may restrict their sense of responsibility to their tribe, clan, or other relatively small social groups because they are not sure of what it means. Some extend their responsibility to all living things, or even to non-living things. For others, it may mean following the scriptures or commandments of a certain religion.

In all these cases, the responsibility is to do the "right" thing, not the easy, safe, or selfish thing, whenever the lives of people, or of other living things, are at stake. For example, if you see an older man fall off a curb, you may hurry to help him up. No one told you to rescue the older man, but you are morally obliged to do so. In the same vein, you may give up your seat on a public bus to a pregnant woman or an older adult without being told to do that. That is moral responsibility. The sense of moral responsibility is found in every person's heart. In the Holy Bible, God told the prophet Jeremiah that He would sign a new covenant with His people so that they would know the difference between right and wrong.

"I will put my law in their minds and write it on their hearts." — Jeremiah 31:33

Many religions and cultural traditions around the world have established norms of behavior, rules, or commandments to guide people in keeping this often-difficult ethical commitment. They usually include things like gratitude to a god; not hurting other people intentionally; dealing fairly without lying, stealing, or cheating; helping others in trouble; and not despoiling the common environment.

A person's moral responsibility is to follow the principles of their moral tradition to the best of their ability, to seek advice when they are having trouble doing so, and to continually seek the most effective outcome for everyone and everything affected by their choices and actions. It is your moral responsibility to behave and generally conduct yourself in such a way that is morally acceptable. For example, you should not take advantage of those who are not able to protect themselves or their possessions or cause pain, suffering, and distress to anyone. In short, do not do to others what you would not wish to be done to you.

Social Responsibility

Social responsibility is the concept that individual people and organizations have a responsibility to act for the benefit of the entire society. This often involves working to strike a balance between economic development and the welfare of the society and environment. In this way, it relates not only to businesses but also to everyone whose action has a direct or indirect impact on the environment. Eliminating barriers to health care to people in rural areas, for example, requires many groups and individuals to work together in a socially responsible way.

Social responsibility can be either passive or active. Passive responsibility means deciding not to engage in socially harmful acts, while active responsibility involves taking actions that contribute directly to the fulfillment of social goals. Social responsibility must also be intergenerational, since the actions of one generation have far-reaching consequences on those who come after them.

We all need to know and learn our responsibilities as citizens for us to better serve our country. We must understand that each of us is responsible for what we do in this country, because we are bound to be affected at some point if the society gets hurt due to our reckless actions. Let's not think that our actions will have no effect on our life. Our collaborative actions and thoughts have many effects on the overall wellbeing of our society. Therefore, our responsibility as good citizens of this country is to care for the society while we work for the unity of its people. However, as we aspire to transform the country we call our own, let's also try to change the society we live in. Try to unite and stay connected to the members of your society.

Our responsibilities as good citizens also include making our society a safer and better place for all of us. We need to live life without fears and concerns for our safety. It is also our collective responsibility to make everything that seems to be impossible become possible and work to make our dreams come true. This cannot happen overnight without determination, education, and a brave heart pushing for it. We are also responsible for making our societal rules fair and applicable to everyone regardless of social class, race, disability, or religion.

Another vital responsibility as good citizens is to make our own living space as clean and organized as possible. We have to be responsible enough to keep our country's environment clean by knowing where we can and cannot throw our garbage to avoid polluting our ecosystem.

If you ever wonder why we should care about our responsibilities as good citizens, you need to ask yourself a question about what your purpose is as a human being in South Sudan. We take absolute responsibility because every action we take will either affect or contribute to the development or wellbeing of our society and country at large. We also have to understand that the society and the country are made by humankind. Our actions, thoughts, and behaviors are going to produce the result if we commit to playing our role. If our country is not a safe place today, it is because some of us are not fulfilling our responsibilities as good citizens. Such failure will have an adverse impact on the life of others.

Our responsibility as good citizens is all about doing good for the country and the societies we represent in all aspects. Since the wellbeing of society and the future of our children depend on us, we have to make sure that we eradicate irresponsibility countrywide.

Should we fail to do that, our children and our children's children will continue to suffer in the end. It is our collective responsibility as good citizens to do good for this country. The country and its social welfare depend on our accumulated actions and ideas. Let's commit to taking on these responsibilities so that we leave behind a better South Sudan for our children and the generations to come.

EPILOGUE

In school, you can be expelled if you are a crook or uncouth. In the military, you cannot get a promotion if you are undisciplined. In the church, a cleric will tell you directly that you will not go to heaven unless you become a good person. In your social life, you cannot have a good friend if you are hard to deal with. Anything crucial under the sun needs humanity to be of ethical conduct to attain it.

Many people blame the worst problems they face in the world on heterogeneity. People think that if they are homogenous, the world could be a conflict-free place suitable for living. This is not correct. I would say each human being is naturally heterogeneous. Every hour, he possesses different thoughts, emotions, and feelings; every day, he changes diets and thinks of different variety of food; and every year, he makes new friends. What he likes today may be different tomorrow. For his own good, he embraces himself and moves on. He controls himself, because if he does not do so, stress, misery, and destruction may besiege him and rob him of his good health. Distress may destroy his happiness empire, which is the throne of his comfort.

Generations will bear witness to the fact that no country has ever been entirely homogeneous, since man himself is not. Language may be the same, but race may be different; culture may be monolithic, but religion may be diverse; and the dress code may be uniform, but choice of color may vary.

Homogeneity cannot be forced; when it was attempted in France, more innocent blood was shed. If you think homogeneity of language is a source of political stability and peace, ask Somalis; if you think religious homogeneity is an answer to the country's problems, why was there uprising in the Arab world? If you think cultural homogeneity is the solution, why was there a deadly genocide in Rwanda?

Nothing found without is as meaningful as what lives within a man's heart. Peace, development, prosperity — all are achieved when citizens understand the meaning of common good. When you speak your own language, have your own culture, maintain your race, and believe in a religion of your choice, you need to work extra hard to respect, value, preserve and protect what is good for all. What is the common good? The common good is what is shared by all citizens: the natural resources, the government institutions that belong to all, the direction of the country and its leadership. In any country, whatever is considered national and for all, that is a common good.

The secret of good citizenship is hidden in the biblical saying, "Do unto others as you would have them do unto you." You need to treat other people in the same way you would expect them to treat you if you were in their place.

Everything under the sun is under the responsibility of a man, although he is not fully aware of it yet. The birds in the sky, the fish in the water, the animals in the bush, and the minerals underground — all belong to him. In his wisdom, he can use them for his own good to rejoice and enrich himself, and in his folly, he can use them against himself to rob himself of his own joy and cause misery and distress. Humankind is created with a purpose to represent the Creator on earth. As a representative, man is expected to be honest, compassionate, disciplined, law-abiding, and peace-loving.

Against all odds, he should have the courage to resist worldly temptations and remain steady in the face of the strongest storms. He is required to pay allegiance and remain loyal to the One who created the universe. His discipline should enable him to treat every creature with respect, his compassion should tell him to lend a helping hand to humanity, his law-abiding nature should help him know the difference between bad and good, and his love for peace should stop him from shedding innocent blood. It is his responsibility to make peace with nature and all its inhabitants.

He has to volunteer to safeguard the world from the abyss of ignorance and weakness of human nature. As I rest my pen, I am so certain the world will one day be a better place when man acknowledges that he is created with a purpose. On that day, our children in the nation of South Sudan will rise up and sing the song of praise, saying:

Thank you God for blessing us with great ancestors
Tall, smooth-skinned and courageous generation
Who witnessed the world's longest civil war
And never gave up the fight for freedom
From slavery and political domination
To religious and racial discrimination

Thank you God for the gift of a great land
Cradle of savanna, swamp and plateau
Blessed with the longest Nile River on earth
And plentiful natural resources of all types
We owe all to the sacrifice of our forefathers
Who laid the foundation of our national unity

One nation with a monolithic vision
Home of lovely and united sixty-four tribes
With diverse creeds, cultures and languages
We find our pride in our rich diversity
Tribalism has no place in our midst
Merit is what defines our choices
Thank you God for the gift of great ancestors

Index

Bibliography

Adekola, Yinusa Adekunle. 2008. Curbing Ganglandism among Nigerian Youths Using Vocational Technical Education as a Veritable Instrument: Case Study of Niger-Delta Youth. Paper presented at proceedings of the 17th Annual African/Diaspora Conference, California State University, Sacramento, CA.

Ali, Nada Mustafa. 2011. "Gender and Statebuilding in South Sudan." United States Institute of Peace, https://www.usip.org/publications/2011/12/gender-and-statebuilding-south-sudan

Allen, James. 1903. *As Man Thinketh*. United Kingdom.

Allen, James. 1901. *From Poverty to Power*. United Kingdom.

Armstrong, Jennifer, and Lisa Dungate. 2011. "The Six Types of Courage." *Lion's Whiskers*, http://www.lionswhiskers.com/p/six-types-of-courage.html

Audi, Robert. 2000. Religious Commitment and Secular Reason. Cambridge, United Kingdom: Cambridge University Press.

Buckeye, Terrence H. 2010. "The Military Role in Reconciliation." School of Advanced Military Studies.

Byman, Daniel L. 2002. *Keeping the Peace: Lasting Solutions to Ethnic Conflicts*. Baltimore, Maryland: The John Hopkins University Press.

Collins, Robert O. 2008. *A History of Modern Sudan*. Cambridge, United Kingdom: Cambridge University Press.

Copnall, James. 2014. *A Poisonous Thorn in Our Hearts: Sudan and South Sudan's Bitter and Incomplete Divorce*. London, United Kingdom: Fountain Publishers.

Deng, Francis M. 1995. *War of Visions: Conflict of Identities in the Sudan*. Washington, DC: The Brookings Institution.

Dozier, Barbra. 2018. "Importance of Discipline among Military Members and Civilians." *Barbra Dozier's Blog*, https://barbradozier.wordpress.com/2018/05/29/importance-of-discipline-among-military-members-and-civilians/

Flamm, Michael. 2005. *Law and Order: Street Crime, Civil Unrest, and the Crisis of Liberalism in the 1960s*. New York: Columbia University Press.

Fogelson, Robert M. 1971. *Violence as Protest: A Study of Riots and Ghettos.* Garden City, New York: Doubleday.

Fox, Jonathan. 2004. Religion, Civilization, and Civil War: 1945 through the New Millennium. Lanham, Maryland: Lexington Books.

Gershon, Livia. 2017. "How People Paid Their Taxes in Biblical Times." *JSTOR Daily,* https://daily.jstor.org/how-people-paid-their-taxes-in-biblical-times/

Haug, Frigga. 2005. "Gender Relations." *Historical Materialism* 13, no. 2: 279-302.

Herb, Guntram H., and David H. Kaplan, eds. 2008. *Nations and Nationalism: A Global Historical Overview.* Santa Barbara, California: ABC-CLIO.

Hoeffler, Anke. 2011. "'Greed' versus 'Grievance': A Useful Conceptual Distinction in the Study of Civil War?" *Studies in Ethnicity and Nationalism* 11, no. 2: 274-284.

Ichijo, Atsuko. 2016. "The Origin of Nationalism." *The State of Nationalism: An International Review,* https://stateofnationalism.eu/article/the-origin-of-nationalism/313/#article

Institute for Economics and Peace. 2017. *Positive Peace: The Lens to Achieve the Sustaining Peace Agenda.*

Johnson, Douglas H. 2011. *The Root Causes of Sudan's Civil Wars: Peace or Truce.* Woodbridge, United Kingdom: Boydell & Brewer.

Jok, Jok Madut. 2007. *Sudan: Race, Religion and Violence.* Oxford, United Kingdom: One World.

Khan, Mushtaq H. 2009. *Governance, Growth and Poverty Reduction.* United Nations, Department of Economics and Social Affairs.

Kimenyi, Mwangi S., John Mukum Mbaku, and Nelipher Moyo. 2010. "Reconstituting Africa's Failed States: The Case of Somalia." *Social Research* 77, no. 4: 1339-1366.

Kingsley, Regeena. 2017. "What are 'Rules of Engagement'? Military Mandates & Instructions for the Use of Force." *Military Caveats,* http://militarycaveats.com/9-what-are-rules-of-engagement/

Kinzer, Stephen. 2004. A Thousand Hills: *Rwanda's Rebirth and the Man Who Dreamed It.* Hoboken, New Jersey: John Wiley & Sons.

Kostić, Roland. 2008. "Nationbuilding as an Instrument of Peace? Exploring Local Attitudes towards International Nationbuilding and Reconciliation in Bosnia and Herzegovina." Civil Wars 10, no. 4: 384-412.

Kriesberg, Louis. 2007. *Constructive Conflicts: From Escalation to Resolution.* 3rd ed. Oxford, United Kingdom: Rowman & Littlefield.

Lamia, Mary C. 2010. "Your Sense of Agency: Are You in Control of Your Life?" *Psychology Today,* https://www.psychologytoday.com/us/blog/the-white-knight-syndrome/201009/your-sense-agency-are-you-in-control-your-life

Little, David, ed. 2007. *Peacemakers in Action: Profiles of Religion in Conflict Resolution.* Cambridge, United Kingdom: Cambridge University Press.

Martin, Harriet. 2006. *Kings of Peace, Pawns of War: The Untold Story of Peacemaking.* London, United Kingdom: Continuum.

Maxwell, John C. 2008. Mentoring 101: What Every Leader Needs to Know. Nashville, Tennessee, Thomas Nelson.

Miller-Idriss, Cynthia. 2016. "The Emotional Attachment of National Symbols." *New York Times,* https://www.nytimes.com/roomfordebate/2016/09/01/americans-and-their-flag/the-emotional-attachment-of-national-symbols

Mugenda, Abel Gitau. 2008. Social Science Research: Theory and Principles: Nairobi, Kenya: Arts Press.

Mutabazi, Sam Stewart. 2019. How to Become a Billionaire in a Third World Country. LAP LAMBERT Academic Publishing.

The New York Times. 1864. "The Public Duty of the Citizen," August 15, 1864, p. 4.

Nhema, Alfred G., and Paul Tiyambe Zeleza. 2008. *The Resolution of African Conflicts: The Management of Conflict Resolution & Post-Conflict Reconstruction.* Addis Ababa and Oxford: OSSREA and James Currey.

Nyong'o, Dorothy. 2013. State Building in South Sudan: Priorities for Development Policy Research. Nairobi, Kenya: African Research and Resource Forum (ARRF).

Rehn, Elisabeth, and Ellen Johnson Sirleaf. 2002. *Women, War, Peace: The Independent Experts' Assessment on the Impact of Armed Conflict on Women and Women's Role in Peace-Building.* New York: United Nations Development Fund for Women.

Taylor, Paul W. 1986. *Respect for Nature: A Theory of Environmental Ethics*. Princeton, New Jersey: Princeton University Press.

Tracy, Brian. 2010. *Goals! How to Get Everything You Want — Faster Than You Ever Thought Possible*. San Francisco, California: Berrett-Koehler.

Wagele, Elizabeth. 2015. "Nine Kinds of Responsibility." *Psychology Today*, https://www.psychologytoday.com/nz/blog/the-career-within-you/201508/nine-kinds-responsibility

Woods, Eric Taylor. 2015. "Cultural Nationalism." *The State of Nationalism: An International Review*, https://stateofnationalism.eu/article/cultural-nationalism/